BE MY love

BE MY love

A Novel

KIT PEARSON

Harper*Trophy*Canada

Published by Harper*Trophy*Canada™,
an imprint of HarperCollins Publishers Ltd

First edition

HarperCollins books may be purchased for educational, business,
or sales promotional use through our Special Markets Department.

HarperCollins Publishers Ltd
Bay Adelaide Centre, East Tower
22 Adelaide Street West, 41st Floor
Toronto, Ontario, Canada
M5H 4E3

www.harpercollins.ca

Library and Archives Canada Cataloguing in Publication
information is available upon request.

Text design by Lola Landekic

ISBN 978-1-4434-4402-6

Printed and bound in the United States of America.
LSC/H 9 8 7 6 5 4 3 2 1

For Maria Chavez
and
Sophie and Charlotte Taylor

The past is a foreign country;
they do things differently there.

—L. P. HARTLEY

GRAND'S FAMILY TREE

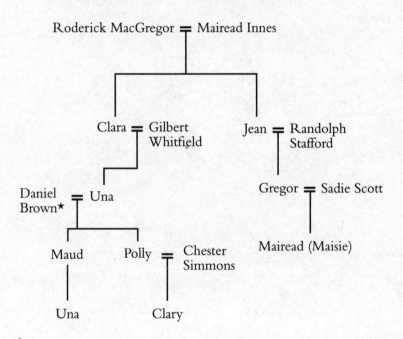

Roderick MacGregor = Mairead Innes

Clara = Gilbert Whitfield

Jean = Randolph Stafford

Daniel Brown* = Una

Gregor = Sadie Scott

Maud

Polly = Chester Simmons

Mairead (Maisie)

Una

Clary

★ Daniel married Esther Meyer after the death of his first wife, Una.

BE MY love

CHAPTER ONE

The Beginning of Summer, 1951

Maisie and her mother were in the car at the Victoria boat terminal. People were starting to board the steamer, but Mum just sat there. "Oh, pickle, how I'll miss you!" she kept saying.

Maisie tried to be patient. She *would* miss her tired, sad mum. But she could hardly wait to get away from her.

"Mum, I should go," she said again.

Her mother wiped her eyes, then finally opened the door and helped Maisie load up. In one hand she held her small suitcase. In the other she balanced a hamper on wheels. It was filled with the items Granny had requested: Indian chutney, Marmite, British magazines, a set of towels, bars of Yardley soap, packets of humbugs, gardening gloves, a new yellow slicker for Grand,

and a huge bag of Scottish steel cut oats. After they'd driven down from Duncan to Victoria early that morning, Mum and Maisie had spent hours ticking off the items on Granny's list.

"Be careful not to tip the hamper—the jars are on top," warned Mum. "Oh, my darling girl . . . what will I do without you?"

"I have to board," said Maisie quickly. She kissed her mother one more time. "I love you, Mum. See you in August!"

"Oh, how I love *you*, pickle!"

Maisie turned to wave from the top of the gang-plank. What a miserable summer her mother was going to have! Maisie shuddered at the thought of the silence that would seep into every corner of the rectory.

But that wasn't her fault! She needed a break. This was *her* time now, the best time of the year: almost the whole summer without her parents, before they arrived on the island for the last two weeks of the holidays.

Maisie waved again from the deck. She knew her mother would stand there until the steamer was out of sight, but after Maisie blew a kiss, she turned her back. Then she hurried to the front of the boat so she could keep watch all the way to the island.

What a relief to feel the cool sea breeze lift her hair! All week it had been so hot that Maisie had slept on a cot in the basement. Yesterday, at her graduation from grade nine, she had sweltered in her black gown. She and Jim had poked each other so much that the principal frowned, but they didn't care. School was done with! No one could make them stay after class or write lines—after the ceremony they were *free*.

Jim . . . Maisie's face burned. All year he had been her good chum. They sat across from each other at the back of the classroom, constantly getting scolded for whispering and playing secret games of cards. Some of the sillier girls said he was Maisie's boyfriend, but he wasn't. He was just a friend: handy for taking to school dances without the tension of being on a real "date."

All Maisie's other friends at her small junior high school were girls, and most of them had been together since grade one. Maisie was constantly attending birthday parties or movies with Lindy or Betty or Ruth or Dawna. They knew and accepted one another.

Lately, however, the girls had changed. Just because they were about to enter high school, they tried to mirror the teenagers in magazines and movies. All they wanted to talk about were Jimmy Stewart and Betty Grable and the latest hairstyles and who had a crush on whom.

Maisie pretended to be interested in all these things, but she really couldn't give a fig about them.

But then had come last night's party and what had happened afterwards ...

Don't think about it! In her mind, Maisie gathered up all her embarrassment about Jim, wrapped it in a tight ball, and threw it into the swirling water.

There! She didn't have to think about anyone at school for two whole months. Anyway, none of them were *real* friends. Her only real friend was her cousin Una. *She* never changed. And very shortly Maisie was going to see her!

The boat sliced like a huge swan through the calm sea, passing the many islands between Victoria and Vancouver. Gulls wheeled overhead, and seals poked up their dark heads, then sank below the waves. The sky was a boundless blue.

Maisie watched impatiently as the steamer docked at Valencia Island and people got off and on. Finally they rounded the point and headed into the choppy water of the pass. As they approached Kingfisher Island, Maisie thirstily drank in every detail: its steep sides blanketed with dark firs, the few houses dotted along the shore, and the lighthouse on the distant point. Her eager gaze found the store, hotel, gas station, and hall that made up the tiny village.

She strained her eyes to see who was waiting on the wharf. Yes, there they were! Granny, in slacks as usual, held a cigarette and bounced with excitement.

Grand stood quietly beside her, the sun glinting on his glasses.

But where was the usual family crowd? Where were Polly and Chester and little Clary, and Maud and Uncle Daniel and Aunt Esther? Most important, where was *Una*?

"*Yoo*-hoo! *Mai*sie!" sang out Granny. Grand waved beside her.

"*Yoo*-hoo! *Gran*ny!"

They always did this. Maisie grinned as the steamer edged up to the end of the wharf. She was *home*.

"It's my bonny wee girl!" cried Granny, kissing Maisie again and again.

Maisie picked up Granny's tiny figure, making her shriek. "It's my bonny wee granny!"

Grand pecked her on the cheek and said quietly, "Welcome back, my dear child."

As usual, Maisie wanted to stroke his perfectly round bald head. "But where *is* everyone?" she asked.

"Oh, chickie, don't you remember? They all had to stay in Vancouver for the weekend to go to Esther's brother's funeral on Monday. I told you that last week on the phone."

Granny must have told Mum, not her. "Even *Una* had to go?"

"Of course! Ben was her great-uncle, after all."

Grand took the hamper. "I suppose he would

be called her *step*-great-uncle, since Esther is her step-grandmother."

"Oh, don't be so pedantic, Rand. Whatever he was, Ben was very fond of Una. What a nice man he was, and what a tragedy he went so soon! Rachel and David must be devastated."

Maisie mumbled a reply, trying to conceal her disappointment.

"Don't worry, chickie." Granny put her arm around Maisie as they walked along the dusty road to the rectory. "You'll see Una on Tuesday, and until then we have you all to ourselves! There's roast chicken for dinner, with strawberry shortcake for dessert—your favourites."

That was more cheerful. So was Granny's non-stop chatter. You didn't have to really listen to her; Grand probably hadn't for years. Her chirpy words were as soothing and safe as a warm bath after coming in from the cold.

⁊ꝺ

The rectory was a simple brown-shingled house with a green roof. Outside were perfectly stacked piles of wood and tidy rows of vegetables and flowers, fenced against the deer. Maisie stepped inside and inhaled the usual delicious odours of damp wood and lavender. She helped Granny wheel the hamper to the kitchen.

"My favourite soap—how lovely!" exclaimed Granny, as if she hadn't requested that they buy it. "And we're just running out of oats. I keep asking Mr. Wynne to order them, but he says that everyone prefers rolled oats. But what's this?" She held up an envelope full of money.

"That's the change from your cheque," Maisie told her.

"But I told your mother to *keep* the change! The Lord knows she and Gregor need every cent they can get these days . . ."

Maisie shrugged. "Well, you know how Mum is—she insisted on giving it to you."

She fled from Granny's tut-tutting and carried her suitcase up to her room under the eaves.

From one window she could see the glittering sea across the road, and from the other the dark firs at the back. There was her narrow bed, covered with the yellow quilt Granny had made for her when she was born. MAIREAD JEAN STAFFORD, DECEMBER 10, 1936 was embroidered on it. There were her comics and her childhood books, including her complete set of Nancy Drews. There was her chest of drawers. On top were a brush and mirror, their silver backs engraved with MJM, for "Mairead Jean MacGregor," Maisie's great-grandmother from Scotland.

Maisie picked up the mirror. Granny kept the back polished, but the glass was pitted and streaky. Maisie frowned at her own chubby face and wild curls, then put down the mirror quickly, wondering as usual what her namesake had been like. One day Granny was going to take her to Scotland to visit her family home.

In a few minutes Maisie had unpacked all her clothes. Every summer she brought the same things: two pairs of jeans, two pairs of shorts, T-shirts, a few sweaters and blouses, and underwear. Mum always tried to sneak in a skirt, and Maisie always took it out. That's what the summer was *for*: to be free of the skirts and dresses she had to wear to school.

On the island the only time she had to wear a skirt was to church or special occasions. Maisie always wore an old kilt in the MacGregor tartan, which had once belonged to her father. She grinned at it in the closet as she hung up her jacket. A kilt was much more fun to wear than a skirt. When she was younger, she used to pretend she was Bonnie Prince Charlie.

She raced downstairs. The kitchen smelled of baking chicken.

"May I help?" asked Maisie.

"Eventually you can—but aren't you going for your swim first?" Maisie's annual ritual was to plunge into the sea as soon as she arrived.

"I can't!" moaned Maisie.

"Oh, poor bairn, have you got your monthlies? Never mind . . . you have all summer to swim. Here—you can shell the peas."

Maisie took them out to the back stoop and went through the familiar motions of splitting pods and scraping the tender green peas into a pot. A raven gurgled, and she could hear the whistle of the departing steamer. Even though she wouldn't see Una until Tuesday, she was at peace.

❧

Granny and Grand had lived in the rectory for over thirty years. He had been born on the island. Granny met him when she and her parents and older sister moved here from Stirling, when Granny was thirteen.

"Your grandfather and I went to school together, but we didn't get along then," Granny had told Maisie. "I thought Rand was too quiet, and he thought *I* was too chatty!"

Grand had gone to theological college in Vancouver, and when he returned to the island to be a curate at the church, he became, as Granny said, "seduced" by her friend Mildred, with whom Granny was in constant competition.

"Once I realized what Mildred was up to, I moved

right in," she said. "She didn't have a chance. She had to settle for Walter, who is such a stick of a man. He may be a doctor, but Rand is far more intelligent."

Maisie and Grand were constantly amused at the rivalry between "Mrs. Doctor Cunningham" and Granny. They were always one-upping each other, from who had the smartest son to who grew the largest pumpkin.

Granny was certainly a better cook than Mrs. Cunningham. Maisie had often eaten there, and the meals were stodgy. Tonight she finished her second helping of shortcake and tried to resist asking for a third. Food was such a comfort—especially when it was this good. At home they ate endless dinners of beans on toast to save money.

"You won't believe what Mildred told me at the store this morning!" said Granny.

"Here we go," said Grand, winking at Maisie.

As usual, Granny ignored him. "She's going to order some new snoods."

"What's a snood?" asked Maisie.

"Don't you remember? It's a long net to keep your hair out of the way. We all wore them during the war, but it's 1951! No one wears snoods anymore. I told Mildred she should cut her hair shorter, and then she wouldn't need one, but of course she won't listen to me."

Maisie helped clear the table and make the tea.

"Now, chickie, tell us about your dear father," said Granny, when they were settled in the living room.

Here it was: the question for which Maisie had been steeling herself all evening. "Dad's just the same," she mumbled.

Grand shook his head. "I just can't understand it! Why would Gregor give up the church so suddenly? I've written him several letters, but he won't answer them, and he refuses to talk about it on the phone."

"Can you tell us exactly what happened?" asked Granny. "We still don't know all the details."

To keep her voice steady, Maisie spoke to the floor. "On Easter Sunday Dad was lifting the bread and wine, but then his arms started shaking. He put them down and just . . . walked out. Everyone started whispering. Mum and I stood there for a few minutes. We didn't know what to do. Then Mr. Linden—he's the warden—told us to go back to the house and said he would ask the organist to play some hymns. We hurried home and found Dad in his study. He wouldn't look at us. When Mum asked him what happened, he said he was going to stop being a rector and that he didn't want to say any more about it."

"Oh, my poor boy!" Granny wiped her eyes.

Grand looked puzzled. "I know your mother took your father to a doctor and that he said Gregor was depressed. But what exactly does that mean?"

"Mum explained it to me. It means that Dad is really, really sad—that he's been like that for a long time."

"It's the bloody war!" said Granny. "It completely changed him. Gregor was such a happy lad before he went over."

"But war saddens everyone," said Grand. "I know Gregor must have seen some terrible things. So did I, in the First World War. Chester was over, and *he's* all right. What did Gregor experience that we didn't?"

"Mum asks him sometimes, but he won't talk about it."

"He wasn't even there for very long," said Grand. "Only a year."

"A year and a *half*," said Granny. "The longest time I've ever lived through! Did the doctor say how we could help him?"

"He said that all we can do is wait for Dad to get better. He's supposed to take a lot of walks, but he doesn't. He just sits in his study all day and pretends to read, or he sleeps on the sofa. It's as if he isn't there!"

"Is it absolutely final, then?" asked Grand. "Has Gregor handed in his resignation?"

Maisie nodded.

"I just can't believe he's given it up," said Grand. "Gregor was a fine rector! He was so good with people, so active—not content just to dabble with books and theology, like me. I had hopes of him becoming a bishop one day."

"You're thinking of him before the war, lovey," said Granny gently. "You know the poor lad hasn't been the same since he came back."

"Yes . . . but I always thought he would get better, not worse." Maisie couldn't bear how disappointed Grand sounded.

"At least they're letting you stay in the rectory until Christmas," said Granny. "But what will you do then?"

"Find another house, I guess." Maisie's voice was getting lower and lower. If only these questions would end! They were like stinging darts.

"But what will you live on? Gregor will just have to find another job," said Granny firmly.

"He *can't* work," said Maisie. "He can barely get up in the morning!" Her voice cracked, and she blinked back tears. She would *not* cry! "Mum says *she'll* find a job. She's waiting until after the summer. The owner of the craft shop says she'll hire her."

"That won't bring in much money," said Granny. "If only your parents could have come with you! It would be much more pleasant for Gregor to be here than moping in his study all day, and I could at least feed them—that would save them money. But when I begged him to come on the phone, he said he wouldn't until his usual time at the end of the summer."

"I asked him, too, but he just kept refusing," said Grand.

Maisie listened to their anguish. What right had Dad to make his parents so miserable? She was *glad* he wasn't here—he would spoil the whole summer!

"Well, maybe when he does come, it will cheer him up," said Grand. "And that doctor can't know what he's suffering spiritually. When Gregor's here, I'll have a little talk with him."

"That's a good idea," said Granny. "I'm sure once he's on the island he'll get over this. He just needs to be back in his childhood home, with lots of fresh air and good food."

Maisie couldn't bear to tell them he wouldn't get over it. Dad's deep gloom was never going to be fixed by a "little talk."

Granny got up and kissed Maisie on the forehead. "Poor chickie—this is all too much for someone your age. At least we have *you* here again. Go to bed now and try not to fash yourself about your father."

Maisie kissed them goodnight. How safe it felt to be told to go to bed! Her legs were so wobbly she could barely climb the stairs.

ಳಿ

The sound of the lapping waves through the open

window usually soothed Maisie to sleep. But the room was hot, and she thrashed and twitched.

Granny was right—all Dad's troubles began with what everyone now called the Second World War. Maisie had been almost three when it started in 1939. She and her parents had just moved to Duncan, where Dad had been appointed the rector of St. Martin's church.

At first the war was simply part of her childhood, like an extra guest at dinner. Maisie was glad that Dad hadn't "gone over," as so many of her friends' fathers had. She assumed that he never would.

It was such a shock, therefore, when he finally enlisted. When Maisie was seven, her father left eagerly for Holland to be the chaplain for a regiment there.

Maisie and her mother had cried all the way home from the boat terminal. They waited eagerly for Dad's letters and read them again and again when they arrived. At first the letters were long and descriptive. Then they suddenly became so short that Mum would search the envelope for more pages. "I guess your dad is just too busy to write more," she said sadly.

Finally the war was over, and at last came the bright fall day when Dad was expected home. Mum got her hair done and bought a new shade of lipstick. Maisie, who was almost nine, was decked out in a horrible pink dress that scratched where it stretched over her middle. She eagerly scanned the people descending the gangplank, watching for a tall man with a cheerful face and a mop of curls like hers.

When Dad appeared, however, his merry curls seemed to be on the wrong face it was so serious and strained. Maisie rushed towards him. Her father used to give her bear hugs, but today it was more like the timid embrace of a teddy bear. He kissed Maisie's mother just as tentatively, and their conversation on the way home was full of silences. Mum's and Maisie's shock and disappointment filled the car like a fog.

"Don't worry—he'll cheer up," Mum kept saying the first week Dad was home. "The poor man is just completely worn out."

But he never did cheer up. Maisie began to think of the golden time before Dad went to war as Before. *Before*, Dad was her jolly, joking companion. They had a trick where she climbed up his thighs while he held her hands and then flipped her over. He had patiently taught her to ride a bike and swim, and to use a hammer and nails in his workshop. Like Mum, he'd called her "pickle"—the name they had given Maisie in the womb, when her mother craved pickles.

Now he never called her "pickle." When he talked to them or preached or had parishioners to dinner, it was as though he was simply going through the motions of being a husband and father and rector.

The worst was Dad's constant irritability. He snapped at them so often that Maisie and Mum learned not to ask him things. Maisie still worked with Dad in his workshop, but his expression was grim as he measured or drilled. She was proud of how obediently the pieces of wood submitted to her cutting and shaping, and she worked hard, desperately grateful for Dad's occasional gruff compliments.

Mum, also, used to brim over with jokes and teasing. Now the carefree mother Maisie had known *Before* had become careworn, instead. It was she who held the congregation together, organizing the altar guild, keeping track of illnesses and anniversaries, and making sure the church was spotless—all the things Granny had taught her when she became engaged to Dad. Granny did all this on the island with boundless energy. Mum, however, always seemed exhausted and dispirited.

Before, their house had rung with laughter. Now Maisie would sit at meals and try to think of something to break the strained silence.

As the years went on, Dad remained the same. He performed all his duties of conducting services and home visiting, but he never went beyond them. He copied his sermons from a book—Maisie had seen it on his desk—and read them so mechanically that people fell asleep. Rectors were supposed to comfort people and offer advice, as Grand did, but Dad tried to put off anyone who came to the door.

He never talked about the war. When Chester told the family stories about his regiment, Dad would look angry and mutter, "That's all over and done with now." But he often had nightmares. Maisie could hear him shouting himself awake, and afterwards Mum's comforting murmurs.

Then Maisie couldn't sleep. She tossed for hours, wondering what had happened to make her father cry out in such agony.

When the Easter disaster happened, everyone in Duncan seemed to know about it, even the ones who didn't go to their church. Some of Maisie's friends asked her curiously what was wrong with her father. Maisie attempted to change the subject, but when they persisted, she tried to explain those strange new words: *depression* and *nervous breakdown*. If only she could tell her friends something more normal, like Dad having a broken leg or the flu!

Mum told her that Dad's depression was *like* having a broken leg or the flu—that he couldn't help being so sad and passive. Maisie couldn't believe that. She wanted to shake him and scream, "*Do* something!"

Mum had to help Dad get dressed and encourage him to eat, as if he were a toddler. Worst of all, the doctor had said that Dad couldn't be left by himself. Mum stayed in the house until Maisie got home from school, then Maisie had to be there while Mum shopped for food.

When Maisie asked why Dad couldn't be alone, Mum just said he would get too lonely. Maisie thought this was ridiculous. Dad barely talked to them—why would it be any different if he was by himself? For three months she had had to cancel all her after-school activities, just to sit in the house with a silent father. And she couldn't have any friends over; it was too embarrassing to have such a weird dad.

Again Maisie thought of how quiet and dreary her house must be now that she was gone. Mum would have no one to talk to, no one to cheer her up.

It was cooler now. An owl screeched as it hunted in the woods. Maisie wanted to sob into her pillow, but that would be being as weak as Dad. *She* was the strong one in the family, and strong people didn't cry. Instead she drew the quilt over her head to make a cave. Then she prayed.

Years ago Grand had told her that the best way to pray was to simply talk to God. "Say whatever you like—how you feel, what you wish for, all your complaints and joys."

So tonight, as usual, Maisie spoke to God in her mind:

Thanks for letting me come to the island again, God. Please make Dad get well. But can't you make them stop asking me about him? And please, *God, let this summer be exactly like all the others.*

CHAPTER TWO

Waiting for Una

When Granny called her, Maisie rolled out of bed and got dressed in her blouse and kilt. She wolfed down some porridge and hurried over to the church to ring the bell. Every summer since she was three that was her job: to pull on the worn leather rope that made the steeple bell clang out over the island.

Today, however, a small freckled boy was waiting in the vestibule with his parents.

"This little chap is very eager to ring the bell—you wouldn't mind letting him have a turn, would you, Maisie?" asked Mr. Francis, the warden.

What could she do but pretend to agree? *It's just a bell*, she told herself as she sat down beside Granny. *Who cares who rings it?* But she always had!

Today was Dominion Day. Maisie listened to Grand

pray for Canada on its eighty-fourth birthday. Normally the two front pews were filled with her family, but now they were crowded with summer visitors. Maisie glanced at them resentfully. This was *their* pew! She and Una usually sat at the end of it, whispering and giggling.

Granny kept the little church sparkling clean. One of Maisie's summer chores would be to help her, but she didn't mind. She liked being in this calm, simple space, with its wooden walls and its clear-glass windows. Visitors were often surprised that they weren't stained, but Maisie liked how the windows brought the outside in.

It was a much more attractive church than Dad's, which had ugly pink walls and concrete pillars. Maisie hadn't been there since Easter. Mum had encouraged her to attend while she stayed home with Dad, but Maisie refused. Everyone would just stare and whisper.

Today she realized how much she missed the familiar service. She never paid much attention to the words, but their old-fashioned cadences had rolled comfortably over her all her life.

Inserted in the wall beside her was a large marble plaque honouring her great-aunt, Clara, Granny's older sister. She had died when Maisie and Una were eleven.

Aunt Clara had been Una's "Nonie," her great-grandmother. She'd looked after Una while Maud, Una's mother, worked in Vancouver. Maud was a lawyer and only came home on the weekends.

Granny had called Aunt Clara "the queen of the island." Everyone admired her and followed her example. She would just *look*, and you would do as she said.

Sometimes Maisie had been the receiver of that look: when she talked with her mouth full or persuaded Una to do something daring, like the time they both climbed onto the roof of the rectory. Maisie had been a bit afraid of Aunt Clara, but Una was her pet. When Aunt Clara died, Una cried so much that she threw up. Maisie had held her and stroked her hair, the way she had sometimes watched Aunt Clara console her.

Granny poked Maisie out of her daydreaming; they were standing up for the final hymn. Then Maisie had to help serve coffee and tea in the church hall, enduring countless handshakes welcoming her back. Across the room she spotted Wendy and Doris, two of Una's friends. She *could* go over and talk to them, but without Una she felt awkward. And they wouldn't welcome her. To them she was a lowly summer visitor, not a real islander.

ৎৡ

That afternoon Grand took the gasboat over to Walker Island to conduct a service there. Maisie chopped kindling and filled the box beside the stove with wood. Then she helped Granny cook dinner for the Cunninghams.

"Wait until Mildred tastes my venison pie," muttered Granny, thumping down pastry on a marble slab. "*Her* crust is always so tough."

Maisie had to put on her kilt again and sit politely while the adults talked about tedious things like the Korean War. Grand had tried to explain to her about this new war, between North and South Korea, but Maisie only pretended to listen. How tired she was of hearing about wars!

Dr. Cunningham asked Maisie about her favourite school subjects. That was even more boring, and Maisie answered as shortly as possible. It wasn't fair to ask about school when it was over!

Granny looked satisfied when Mrs. Cunningham praised the pie and the rhubarb crisp. But then she began boasting about her son, Alec, who was a businessman in Ottawa.

"And how is *your* dear son?" she asked sweetly.

Granny winced. "As well as can be expected, thank you."

Maisie's cheeks burned. The whole island must know! Mrs. Cunningham tossed her head with an expression of superiority and pity—as if there were something shameful about Dad.

❧

Monday was unbearably long. Grand retreated to his study as usual, and Granny had one of her headaches.

"I'm going to have a wee lie-down, chickie," she said after breakfast. "Why don't you make yourself a sandwich and go out and play. Be sure to take your hat—it's going to be a scorcher again. Stay in the shade as much as you can. You know how easily you burn."

Maisie bristled. She was fourteen and a half—much too old to "go out and play"! And she didn't have to be told how to protect herself from the sun. As usual, Granny treated her as if she were still a little child. Grunting a reply, she packed herself a cheese sandwich, an apple, and three chocolate chip cookies. She pushed her lunch into a knapsack, crammed on her favourite old blue hat, and decided to walk to the lighthouse.

Maisie knew every beach and road and rock on Kingfisher, and almost every one of its 180 inhabitants. As always, however, the island was so quiet it seemed deserted. The only life she encountered was a doe and two tiny new fawns in the ditch, reaching up to nibble goatsbeard blossoms. The mother tried to persuade the fawns to cross the road. Finally they darted nervously after her.

Una used to yearn to stroke a fawn and would spend hours outside in a chair, trying to entice one with a piece of apple. Once, a doe approached and took it, but never a fawn.

Maisie found some wild strawberries and nibbled on them as she trudged along. How hot it was! Wiping the sweat from under her hat, she decided to turn back and go to the beach, instead. She headed for the rocky shore in front of the rectory. At the far end was a shady patch of sand, under the low overhanging branches of a huge arbutus. This was one of Maisie and Una's secret spots. When they were little, they'd bounced on the branches and pretended they were horses, or made forts out of the driftwood that littered the sand.

Maisie leaned against a log and ate all her cookies. She watched an otter roll and dive as it fished offshore. Then it swam out too far to be seen. At least *it* was allowed to swim.

The water looked so clear and green against the grey rocks. Maisie took off her sandals and paddled, but that just made her long to go right under. *Boys* didn't have to endure this monthly restriction . . . it was so unfair!

What could she do? Maybe go to the Hut . . . but she wanted to save that for Una. *Nothing* seemed worth doing without her cousin. Maisie felt so empty and listless it scared her. This was how Dad must feel all the time.

But she *wasn't* Dad! She forced herself to get up and walk briskly along the road to the wharf. Little Bobby and Lennie Maclean were fishing at the end of it. Maisie sat with them, the boards rough under her thighs. Many small fishing boats were in the pass, with crowds of gulls screaming over them.

"Look, Maisie!" said Lennie.

A cod flopped in a bucket. While Maisie was admiring it, Bobby caught another.

"We're going to sell them to the hotel," he said.

"The hotel is closed until Wednesday," she told them. "My uncle and aunt have gone to a funeral in Vancouver."

"Wednesday! But that's too late! Mrs. Brown won't buy fish unless they're fresh."

"You'll just have to take them home," said Maisie. "I'm sure your mother will be glad to have them."

"Yeah, but she won't *pay* us," grumbled Bobby.

Looking downcast, the two boys packed up their gear and trudged away.

Maisie ate the rest of her lunch sitting on the coronation seat above the wharf. It was an octagonal bench built around a young beech tree that had been planted when King George VI had been crowned in 1937.

Two years later, on the royal visit to Canada, Granny had stood with other islanders at Otter Point to wave to the king and queen's boat on its way to Victoria. Granny insisted that the queen had waved back.

After she'd eaten, Maisie wandered over to the store to buy a Coke. Susan and Glen Wade were sitting on the bench outside it, sharing a bag of chips.

"Hiya, Maisie," said Glen lazily.

Glen's greasy hair and pimpled face repulsed Maisie. She ignored him and said hello to his sister. Sometimes Susan hung around with her and Una, even though she was two years younger.

Susan just grunted a reply, then asked "When's Una coming back?"

"Tomorrow," said Maisie. Like the girls at church, Susan wasn't going to be friendly unless Una was there.

If only she *were* a real islander! Mum had once told her that Granny and Grand had invited her and Maisie to live with them while Dad was in the war, but Mum had said she didn't want to be beholden to them. Imagine being here all year, living in the rectory and seeing Una every day!

Granny had told Maisie how upset the islanders had been when the Japanese people on the island had been evacuated in 1942. Her good friends, the Okadas, had to leave along with seven other families.

"But why?" Maisie had asked.

Granny looked bitter. "Because they were regarded as enemy aliens. What nonsense—they were Canadians!"

Maisie had a dim memory of her and Una playing with a mischievous little girl named Mika. Where was she now? How awful to have to leave her home and live in a camp in the interior!

So many children had left the island that the school had closed until 1944. Una was supposed to start grade one that fall, so for two years she and a few of her classmates had been tutored by Grand. If Maisie had lived here, she could have shared that. What bliss!

"Hey, Maisie, whatcha daydreaming about?" jeered Glen.

Maisie fled into the store. It was stuffed with everything anyone would want, from fishing lures to magazines to dishes. She went over to the pop dispenser and fished out a Coke from the icy water.

"Why, hello there, Maisie!" said old Mr. Wynne, the storekeeper. "Welcome back! Shall I put this on your grandmother's tab as usual?"

"Yes, please." He opened the bottle, and Maisie guzzled down the dark, sharp-tasting liquid. Mum didn't like her to drink Coke; she thought it was bad for her teeth. But Mum wasn't here.

"Where's your cohort?" asked Mr. Wynne.

"In Vancouver," Maisie told him, eyeing the candy. She chose Twizzlers, jujubes, and an Almond Joy chocolate bar, and laid them on the counter. Eating this much candy was also forbidden at home, as well as being too expensive. What a treat to be able to indulge herself! Granny never questioned how much Maisie spent.

"Oh, yes, they all went to that funeral," said Mr. Wynne. "You must be lonely without Una—I never see the two of you apart."

"Mmm . . ." Maisie pocketed the candy and turned away so Mr. Wynne wouldn't see her sudden tears.

What was the matter with her? Was Maisie so dependent upon Una that she couldn't amuse herself for just one day?

Stop moping! she told herself. She decided to go home and have some of the leftover crisp. Surely that would cheer her up.

Next door to the rectory was where Una lived, in a large white house with a blue roof. As Maisie approached it, she had an irresistible urge to go up the path to its front door. Then she pushed it open—no one on the island locked any doors—and went inside.

What a relief to be here! The curtains were drawn against the sun, so the house was dim and cool. Maisie knew this living room as well as Granny's, but it couldn't be more different from the rectory's tidy space. Dominated by a huge blackened fireplace, it overflowed with worn fat armchairs, stuffed book-shelves, and many photos in tarnished silver frames. Clary's toys and clothes were scattered on the floor and chairs, and a small glass stood on a plate, encrusted with milk and surrounded by crumbs.

Maisie went upstairs. Una's room was in the attic like hers, but it was much larger. Two white iron beds were in it, each with a fluffy sheepskin mat beside it. Maisie had spent countless nights sleeping in the far bed.

She walked around with a mixture of guilt and ownership. Of course she shouldn't be snooping, but this felt like her room as much as Una's. Surely Una wouldn't mind if Maisie came up here—would she?

What Maisie saw made her frown. The top of Una's chest of drawers had always displayed her col-lection of china horses, but they had disappeared. Now it was covered with bobby pins, a compact, eye makeup . . . even a tube of lipstick! On the walls were pinned some of the glossy photographs of movie stars and singers that the girls in Maisie's class were always sending away for.

Quivering with guilt, Maisie opened Una's closet. Una's school uniform was hanging there, along with other clothes she knew. But what was this? Two cot-ton dresses, one pink and one green, in the new full-skirted style. More full skirts . . . even a crinoline!

And, on the floor of the closet beside Una's saddle shoes, a pair of pumps with little heels!

Now a kind of desperate recklessness overcame Maisie's guilt. She opened a drawer. There lay nylons and garter belts, a pink gingham two-piece bathing suit—and a padded brassiere!

Maisie was so shocked that she had to sit down on one of the beds. Leaning against the wall and cramming jujubes into her mouth, she tried to absorb this new information.

Until last year Una had lived in the hotel with her grandparents during the week and attended the tiny school on the island. On some weekends she would go to Vancouver to be with her mother, Maud. On other weekends, and every holiday, Una and Maud would live in this house, which they had inherited from Aunt Clara. It belonged to Polly, as well, but she only came here in the summers with her husband and child.

But since the island school only went up to grade eight, last fall Una had gone to live with her mother in Vancouver. There she had started attending Ashdown Academy, a private girls' school. Her letters had told Maisie every detail about her new friends there. They sounded hoity-toity to Maisie: one had her own horse, and another went to Hawaii every winter holiday.

Una liked most of her teachers, and she had discovered she was an excellent tennis player. Her music teacher encouraged her talent at the piano. "There's so much to do in the city compared with the island!" she had written to Maisie. "Movie theatres and concerts and a swimming pool and lots of stores."

All this had made Maisie nervous, especially hearing about the new friends. But when she had seen her cousin at Christmas, Una was the same as she had always been. Her room was the same, as well. They'd spent much of Christmas week up here, escaping the adults and playing Monopoly.

But what about now? Maisie glanced around. The handsome faces of Mario Lanza and Perry Como seemed to mock her. Was Una turning into a frivolous teenager like Maisie's friends in Duncan? If so, would she still like Maisie?

Even though she was stuffed with jujubes, Maisie unwrapped the chocolate bar. But after a few bites she put it down, feeling sick. She had invaded her best friend's privacy and found out things about her she didn't want to know.

It serves you right for prying, Maisie thought savagely. Now, instead of being impatient for Una's arrival, she dreaded it.

CHAPTER THREE

Nancy and George

As usual on boat days, there was a small crowd on the wharf waiting for their mail. "You're a quiet lass this morning," said Granny. "Are you excited about having Una back?"

Maisie nodded, even though she was terrified. *Please, God, let Una be the same*, she prayed, as the *Queen Mary* drew up.

Suddenly the family was upon her. "Maisie! How lovely to see you after so long!" Many pairs of arms hugged her at the same time. It was like being in the embrace of a friendly octopus.

For a moment Maisie could hardly distinguish between them. Polly, Chester, Clary, Uncle Daniel . . . but not Maud, who had to work and wouldn't be here until the weekend. And not Aunt Esther, who had stayed in Vancouver with her brother's family. But where was Una? Surely not this glamorous-looking teenager.

"Hi, George!" she whispered, kissing Maisie's cheek.

It *was* Una! Maisie managed to croak, "Hi, Nancy." At least they were still using their secret names for each other.

But Una looked like she was in disguise. Her formerly straight hair curled softly around her cheeks, and she wore a chic swirly dress, silver sandals, and red lipstick. The seams on her nylons were as straight as pencils, and there were small butterfly designs on the heels.

Maisie couldn't bear to look at her and turned to the others. Everyone was talking at once; they were the noisiest group on the wharf.

"How was the funeral?" Granny asked.

"It was beautiful," said Polly.

"Who's *that*?" demanded Clary, pointing at Maisie.

Polly laughed. "Oh, Clary, what a silly! This is your cousin Maisie! Don't you remember her from Christmas? She's going to babysit you this summer while Daddy and I work."

Maisie couldn't help smiling. How Clary had changed! At Christmas you couldn't understand her, but now she chatted clearly. It was as if she had finally become a real person.

"I don't *want* a babysitter," said Clary.

Chester laughed. "Don't listen to her, Maisie. She's become very contrary now that she's two and a half, haven't you, Clary?"

"I'm *not* contrary!"

This made all of them laugh. Clary looked indignant and marched away. Chester went after her, and the rest of them followed to the road.

"Have you had a good year at school, Maisie?" Uncle Daniel asked, as they paused at the hotel. He was such a silent, awkward man, but always kind.

Maisie shrugged. "I guess so." School belonged to another time.

He smiled. "We're so glad to have you back on the island. You and Una are going to have a fine summer."

No, we aren't—Una has already ruined it! thought Maisie . . . but of course she couldn't tell him that.

"Dinner's at six!" Granny called, as Uncle Daniel headed to the hotel.

Now there was no choice but to walk with Una. They lingered behind the others. Maisie had to say *something*. "How—how *was* the funeral?"

"It was really interesting—I've never been to a Jewish funeral before. The family wore torn black ribbons to show their grief. And there weren't any flowers. Afterwards we went to the house where they're staying to sit shiva—that involves bringing food and being with the mourners. *Shiva* means 'seven'—people will come over to visit David and his mother and Bubby for seven days. He explained it all to me. I feel *so* sorry for him, losing his dad."

As usual, Una twitched with nervous energy. She kept putting her fingers to her mouth, as if still chewing on the end of one of the braids she used to have.

"Why wasn't the funeral in Boston?" asked Maisie.

"Uncle Ben wanted to be buried in Vancouver with his parents. David was really close to him—I can't imagine how awful he must feel."

Maisie hadn't thought about David Meyer for years. He and his parents used to come often to the hotel that Uncle Daniel and Aunt Esther owned. All day he'd be off with some boys his age, and Maisie and Una would only see him at family gatherings in the evenings. Even at those he practically ignored them.

Then he and his parents moved to Boston. Sometimes his parents came back to visit, but David never accompanied them.

"Is David still snooty?" Maisie asked.

"No! He was really friendly, even though he's so sad. He and I took our food out to the back porch and talked for ages. He goes to Harvard now—he wants to be an astronomer! Isn't that interesting?"

"Mmm . . ." Maisie didn't give a hoot about David. She finally blurted out her question: "Nancy, what have you done to your *hair*?"

Una laughed. "I got a Toni! Mum finally let me. Now it's as curly as yours is!" She leaned over so their heads were touching. "'Which twin has the Toni?'" she asked in a singsongy voice like the one in the commercial.

Granny stopped walking and turned around. "It's obvious that *you* have the Toni, Una. Maisie's curls are *natural*. You shouldn't tamper with the hair the good Lord gave you."

"Yes, Aunt Jean." When Granny moved on, Una rolled her eyes.

Maisie didn't laugh. "What's the matter?" said Una. "Don't *you* like my hair, either?"

The two of them had always been totally honest with each other. "No, I don't!" said Maisie. "And Granny's right. You shouldn't change your hair, because it was fine before—it was beautiful! Now you look too different. And why are you wearing such fancy clothes? And lipstick!"

Una looked huffy. "Well, I *have* just come from the city. And Mum lets me wear lipstick for special occasions. Bubby doesn't approve, but I don't care. I'm almost fifteen, after all. Sometimes, when I go to a matinee with my friends, I even wear eyeshadow!"

Maisie cringed, as she remembered the makeup on the chest of drawers. What would Una think of her if she knew Maisie had snooped in her room?

Una examined Maisie. "I could lend you some, if you like."

"Lend me what?"

"Lipstick! It would look good on you."

"Yuck! *I'll* never wear that stuff!"

Una laughed. "Oh, George, you never change."

Her tone was affectionate, but Maisie felt as if she were being treated like a younger sister.

࿐

Maisie was invited for lunch. Polly made delicious salmon sandwiches, but Clary wouldn't eat hers and demanded cheese. Her needs and chatter dominated the meal, and Maisie sat silently, observing Una.

Except for her ridiculous hairstyle, Una was just as beautiful as ever. Her grey eyes were flecked with bits of green and framed with fine dark eyebrows. She had high cheekbones and full lips. Her muscular but slim body was as perfect as her face. Unlike Maisie, she was quite flat chested—but not today: she must be wearing one of her padded bras.

Granny thought Maisie was the beautiful one: "You're my bonny lass," she was always saying. In her childhood photos Maisie looked like Shirley Temple, with blond curls and a round face. The girls at school envied her hair; at least *she* would never need to have a perm. But now her face was *too* round, along with her bottom and thighs. And her feet were *huge*! Granny and Mum kept saying that Maisie would slim down as she got older. That didn't seem to be happening.

But I'm strong! thought Maisie. *I can lift a whole basket of wood. And carry two pails of water at once.*

"Would it be all right if you start babysitting tomorrow?" asked Polly, after Chester had taken a protesting Clary away for her nap.

Maisie shrugged. "Sure." This was the second summer she'd looked after Clary in the mornings while her parents worked. They paid well, and she earned enough for her spending money all year. She was proud to be able to tell Dad that he didn't need to give her an allowance anymore. His salary wasn't large, and now that he wasn't working his money must be running out.

Then what would happen? But Maisie refused to think of Dad. Polly was telling her what she'd been painting.

"You'll have to come and look, Maisie, and tell me what you think. I'm doing only trees, especially arbutus. I love their vivid colours."

"They don't really look like trees," said Una. "They're called abstracts."

Polly was an artist. After she and Maud inherited the house, she had a studio built behind it. She was getting to be well known, and sometimes people came over to the island to buy one of her paintings.

Polly was just as beautiful as Una, but in a more ethereal way. Her blond hair was so long she could sit on it, although she usually kept it in a braid. No other woman on the island had hair below her shoulders, but Polly didn't care about style. She refused to wear makeup, and she dressed in brightly embroidered smocks and sturdy sandals—Granny called her a bohemian. Clara never wore pastel colours, the way other toddlers did. She was either in tiny red or purple smocks like her mother's, or she ran around in just her underpants or often wore nothing at all.

Polly poured them some tea. "I'm reading an amazing novel, called *From Here to Eternity*. It's all about Pearl Harbor. How strange that such recent events are now considered history! It seems like yesterday that it happened. And then of course so many Japanese families had to leave Kingfisher—that was such a tragedy." Polly sighed. "I still *hate* the war! It's changed so many people, including Chester. Everyone thinks he's the same, but sometimes he wakes up weeping. He's so serious now."

Maisie was surprised: to her, Chester seemed unchanged. But at least he still *acted* normal; at least he made an effort—unlike Dad.

Polly seemed to read her mind. "Of course, your poor father was far more affected. Your mum told us what happened at Easter. How *is* Gregor, Maisie?"

Maisie clenched her hands. "Just the same," she murmured.

Polly smiled at her. "You don't want to talk about him, and I don't blame you. I can't *imagine* what it's like for you and Sadie to live with such sadness! It must be a relief for you to have a break."

Polly was only fourteen years older than Maisie and Una, and the only grown-up who spoke to them like equals. Maisie smiled back and took another cookie.

Chester returned to the living room. "I *think* Clara is down for the count. She insisted on six stories. If we're lucky, we'll get two hours. I'm going to work a bit on my book." Chester taught biology at the University of British Columbia. For the past few summers he'd been writing a book about algae.

"What about you, my precious love? Are you going to paint?" he asked.

He gazed at Polly with such affection, the way Maisie's father used to gaze at her mother . . . *Before.* Maisie winced. Would he ever do so again?

Polly yawned. "We got up so early this morning

I think I'll have a nap, too. What are you girls going to do?"

"Let's go swimming," said Una.

"Not until an hour after lunch," warned Chester.

"We'll sit on the beach, then. All right, Maise? I'll get changed and meet you at your house."

Maisie cheered up. Once Una was back in her normal clothes, surely her real self would be back, as well.

CHAPTER FOUR

A Secret

Maisie had forgotten about the pink two-piecer: a small halter top and a skirt that was so short it only reached the top of Una's legs. At least it didn't have a padded bra, and at least Una had washed off her lipstick.

As for herself, she was wearing the ugliest bathing suit in the world. It was the only one she and Mum had been able to find that fit: an orange-and-black plaid affair with pleats across the tummy. The straps had metal fasteners that dug into her skin. Maisie had wanted to keep on wearing her old black bathing suit, but Mum threw it out because it bagged too much and was dotted with holes.

Never mind . . . today she could finally swim! As soon as they reached their secret spot, Maisie rushed into the sea, gasping as she went deeper—the water was always freezing in July. But she struck out vigorously, her arms doing a steady crawl. In the water Maisie no longer felt lumpish and awkward. She was as strong and streamlined as a seal, her obedient muscles carving through the waves. Out, out she went, not tiring. Then she lay on her back, spread out her arms, and drifted, closing her eyes and letting the sun dry her wet face. She swam in slowly doing the breaststroke.

Una had only dipped. "We forgot to wait an hour—do you think we'll get cramps?"

"That's such a stupid rule," scoffed Maisie. "I've often swum right after a meal, and nothing has ever happened."

They sat in the sun to warm up, eating the cookies Maisie had brought. Her icy skin tingled deliciously. Now her real island self was back.

"Okay, George, tell me everything that's happened since Christmas," demanded Una.

"I already *have* told you," said Maisie. "Didn't you get my letters? You only answered twice!"

Una looked ashamed. "Sorry. School was so busy this term and we got so much homework that I didn't have time to write."

How could she not have time to write a letter? But Maisie let it pass. The sea was a glorious blue, and no one else was on the beach. At last she had Una to herself.

"I loved getting your letters," Una continued, "but you never told me about your dad. Mum says he's stopped being a rector."

"Oh, Nancy . . ." Maisie sat up straighter and faced her. "It's just . . . *horrible*!"

Then she told her everything, all about Easter Day and the long, silent, agonizing time since then. Una had always been a good listener. She let her talk it all out without interrupting.

"Do you think he'll *ever* get better?" asked Maisie. Her voice shook. Una moved next to her and rubbed her shoulder. Maisie leaned against her warm body, her misery shot with relief. They were pals again!

Una gave her a strange look. "I wonder what *my* dad is like now? He'd be thirty-four, like Mum."

Maisie sat up abruptly. "What are you talking about? Your dad is dead!"

Una looked so intense. What was the matter?

"Maisie . . ."

Her voice was so serious!

"I'm going to tell you a *huge* secret. I'm not supposed to, but I don't care. You're my best friend, and it's about time you knew."

"Best friend" . . . those words were so welcome that Maisie didn't care what the secret was. She wrapped her towel around her so she wouldn't burn. "Okay, fire away."

"My dad *is* alive!"

"What? What on earth do you mean, Una? Mum told me he died in a car accident before you were born."

Una nibbled on her finger. "He didn't—he's alive. My father's name is Robert, and he probably lives in Vancouver. He and Mum went out together in first year at U.B.C., and she got into trouble." Una grimaced. "He refused to get married, and he didn't want me. So she decided to have nothing to do with him and to have me out of wedlock. Before I was born, she planned to give me up for adoption, but as soon as she saw me, she loved me so much that she couldn't."

Una heaved a stone into the water, then turned to face Maisie. Her voice quivered. "So, I'm illegitimate. What do you think about *that*, George? Your friend Nancy is a bastard! Do you mind?"

Maisie hugged her. "Of course not!"

But she felt stunned. *Got into trouble, illegitimate, out of wedlock* . . . what did those words mean? *Bastard* was something bad that boys called to each other on the playground, but she didn't know what it meant, either.

How ignorant she was compared with Una! "Can you explain a bit more?" she asked.

Una told her the whole story. Maud had brought Una back to the island soon after she was born. They lived with Aunt Clara—Una's great-grandmother—until Una was three, then Una lived alone with her while Maud went first back to university and then to work as a lawyer. The whole island knew that Maud was an "unmarried mother," but Aunt Clara had quickly quelled anyone who brought it up. "I don't think Aunt Jean ever really approved, but of course she always gave in to Nonie."

So that's why Granny sometimes seemed disapproving of Una! Maisie had always thought it was just because Aunt Clara and Granny had been so competitive about the two girls. Granny had always been quick to point out to her sister how Maisie learned to swim first or what a picky eater Una was. Now Maisie knew it was more than that.

"They all lied to me!" said Maisie angrily. "I'm the only one in the family who didn't know!"

Una looked apologetic. "They thought you were too young. I was supposed to wait until you were eighteen to tell you, but I don't care—I hate having secrets from you!"

Maisie listened, spellbound, as Una continued her story.

"One day when I was nine, Glen whispered to me that I was a bastard. I asked Mum what it meant. She was furious! She told Nonie, and Nonie talked to Glen's parents, and he had to apologize to me."

"But what *does* it mean?"

"It's a swear word for being illegitimate, which

means your parents weren't married when you were born. Mum explained it all to me." Una giggled. "But first she had to explain sex! So I knew a lot when I was nine, more than the other kids."

"You knew about sex when you were *nine*? You never told me!"

Una blushed. "Mum said not to, that you weren't ready yet. But at least you know about it now."

Sometimes on sleepovers they had whispery conversations about intercourse. Una was much more curious about it than Maisie was. Mum had told her the facts of life two years ago. The whole idea was so icky that Maisie hoped she would never have to have anything to do with it.

Una continued. "People on the island have been pretty good about not talking about me. Nonie trained them well! Sometimes Glen mouths that word to me, but I just ignore him."

Maisie was furious—how dare he hurt Una! "I despise Glen! If he ever does it again, tell me, and I'll punch him!"

"Don't be ridiculous—Glen is far bigger than you are. And girls can't beat up boys."

"*I* could!"

"Calm down, George. I haven't finished yet—don't you want to hear the rest?"

Maisie made herself listen.

"Last year, when I went to school in Vancouver, Mum decided we had to make up a story. She *hates* lies, but she said it was necessary. So if any of the girls ask, I tell them what your mother told you—that my father died before I was born. That's what Mum always says at work, as well. She just says she 'lost her husband.' She calls herself 'Mrs. Brown' and jokes that they both had the same last name. She wouldn't have been able to get into such a good law firm if they'd known I was illegitimate."

"But I don't understand—why is it wrong? It's not *your* fault you were born!"

"Well . . . it's my parents' fault. You *know* you're not supposed to have intercourse before you're married. Mum has drilled that into me. She said she made a mistake . . . but she also says that it was the best mistake she ever made!"

But wasn't it *God* who made the mistake? Wasn't *He* the one who decided when children would be born? This sounded so childish, however, that Maisie didn't say it out loud.

She tried to think of something in reply. "Do your friends at school *believe* you when you tell them your father is dead?" she finally asked.

"Sure! Some of them say how sorry they are, but I just shrug and tell them I can't miss him because I can't remember him. That's true!"

"But you know his name."

"Just his first name, Robert. Mum says that when I'm twenty-one, she'll tell me his whole name, and then I can try to find him if I want. She knows where his parents used to live, and maybe they're still there. But I don't want to—I *never* want to find him! He didn't want me, and he abandoned Mum when she needed him the most!"

Now Una's beautiful eyes were welling. Maisie was glad to have another excuse to hug her. Then they sat in silence for a while before they gathered up their things and left the beach.

It was going to take a while to digest this news. Una's revelations made Maisie feel embarrassed about being so innocent. But she was also overjoyed that Una chose *her*, her best friend, to confide in.

❧

All through the large family dinner Maisie thought of Una's secret. Perhaps that explained why Una was always so jumpy and always trying to please every-one—as if she had a fault. But she didn't! Maisie watched how fondly they all looked at Una tonight, how affectionately they responded to her laughing chatter. Even Granny couldn't resist her.

"Aunt Jean, you've outdone yourself!" Una said,

after she'd tasted the cod casserole. "Can you give my mum the recipe?"

Granny beamed. "Of course! I can't believe you're finally liking fish, chickie!"

Una was *treasured*. Treasured and protected, in the hope that she wouldn't suffer from any stigma.

If only she wouldn't! *Maisie* wanted to protect her. She still felt like beating up horrible Glen. But most of all, she wanted to beat up Robert. Imagine not wanting to marry Maud and not wanting the baby he had started with her! *He* was the one who was a bastard!

Maisie was so shocked at her thoughts that she was relieved when Chester came and sat beside her after dinner. "How is your father, Maisie?" he asked gently.

Chester was Dad's best friend—or he was before Dad stopped relating to any friends at all. He was younger than Dad, but they'd both grown up on the island. Maisie remembered the night a few summers ago when Mum asked Chester what had happened to Dad to make him so distant. Everyone else had gone to bed, but Mum didn't know Maisie was reading in the chair in the corner—the same chair she was sitting in now. They had been on the veranda, but she could hear every word.

"What *happened* over there, Chester?" Mum had asked.

There was so much pain in her voice. "Gregor is a completely different person! He goes through all the motions, but underneath he's so *angry*. But he won't tell me why."

"I don't see what would have happened that didn't happen to any of us," Chester replied. "We had a job to do, and often it was a dirty one, but we just got on with it. Of course, we were in different regiments, so I don't know what Gregor experienced. I'm sorry, Sadie, but that's all I can tell you."

Now Maisie grimaced at Chester's kind, concerned face. Once again, she explained that Dad didn't want to be a rector anymore and that the doctor said he was depressed.

"That's what your grandmother told us. I'm so sorry, Maisie. This is very difficult for you and your mother. But she and your dad will be here in August as usual, right?"

Maisie nodded.

"Coming home will do him good. And I'll have a talk with old Gregor while he's here. I bet I can shake him out of this."

That was Chester in a nutshell. He was a nice man, but he was *too* nice. Everything had an easy solution.

Poor Dad . . . first Grand was going to talk him out of his depression and now Chester. Maisie knew that was impossible, but she smiled at Chester and thanked him.

"Come and help me do the puzzle," called Una.

She gave Maisie's hand a quick squeeze, and they exchanged a secret look. Una was wearing one of her silly dresses again, but now Maisie knew that underneath she was still her best friend.

Around them the family buzzed happily. Uncle Daniel was telling Clary "The Three Billy Goats Gruff." He was such a good storyteller; Clary's eyes were round with thrilled terror as he roared, "'Who's *that* walking over my bridge?'"

"Not so wowd, Grandad—Mickey might get afraid," she told him. Mickey was her imaginary friend, named after the famous mouse.

What a hodgepodge of grandparents and aunts and uncles and cousins! When Maisie was little, she had trouble sorting them all out. Then Grand had drawn her a family tree, and now Maisie was proud that she knew all its complications:

Aunt Clara had had one daughter, Una, who was Maud and Polly's mother and had been Maisie's father's first cousin.

Una had married Uncle Daniel very young and had died when Polly was two. Aunt Esther was Uncle Daniel's second wife.

Maud and Polly were Maisie's second cousins, and Una and Clary were first cousins to each other.

Una was Maisie's "second cousin once removed," as was Clary.

All Maisie cared about was that she and Una were related, however distantly. That meant they would always know each other.

Now she knew more about the family than a diagram: a secret that no one ever talked about. *Someone should have told me!* she thought.

But would she have wanted to know before now? She *had* been too young, Maisie realized—just as Clary was.

Anyhow, Una's secret didn't make any difference. Despite some undercurrents of tension, they were a happy family—except for Mum and Dad, but they weren't here.

Here, Maisie was as safe and cherished as Una. And they had the whole summer to look forward to!

CHAPTER FIVE

The First Week

When Maisie walked over the next morning, she could hear Una practising: scales that rippled up and down, each concluded by a resounding chord. How skilled she was!

"Good morning, Maisie—you're right on time!" Polly was waiting on the veranda. Her painting smock was covered with so many dabs of colour that it looked like a painting itself.

Clary, wearing nothing at all, was colouring, although it was more like jabbing the crayons into the paper. Polly addressed her nervously. "Now, sweetheart, remember what I said? Maisie is going to look after you while Mummy and Daddy work."

"No, she isn't," said Clary calmly.

"Of course she is! You two are going to have so much fun!" Polly turned to Maisie. "She may fuss at first, but I'm going to stay in my studio. Chester is writing in the spare bedroom—I've told him to ignore her, as well. Be sure she wears a hat if you go to the beach. I'll see you at lunchtime, pumpkin."

"NO!" Clary ran over to Polly and clutched her legs. "I don't *want* Maisie to wook after me! I only want *you*!"

"Now, Clary, we've already talked about this. You and Maisie are going to have a wonderful time." Polly kissed her, then dashed out to the studio.

Clary emitted such a loud shriek that Maisie was sure the whole island could hear. Una rushed out of the living room. "I can't practise with this racket! *Stop* it, Clary!"

Clary just screamed louder. She picked up her crayons and heaved them into the bushes.

"That's naughty!" Una looked at her small cousin hopelessly, then at Maisie. "Can't you *do* something?"

"I want *Mummy!*" cried Clara. She headed to the door.

"*WAIT!*" shouted Maisie. In the breath between one scream and the next she nattered, "Do you like *cake*? I'm going over to the rectory to help my grand-mother bake a *cake*. You can come if you want."

"Cake? What kind?"

"Chocolate. And Granny *may* let you lick the beaters. She doesn't let screaming girls lick them, though."

Clary frowned. "*I'm* not a screaming gurr."

Maisie dashed into Clary's room, grabbed some clothes, and thrust them on Clary. Then she led the little girl down the veranda stairs.

"Bye-bye, Una," called Clary, now completely cheerful.

The scales stopped. "Bye! Maisie, you are a wonder! I'll see you after lunch." Una had a job, as well. Every morning after she practised she went to the hotel to help clean rooms.

Luckily Granny really was making a cake that morning. "Well, look who's here—my wee chickie!"

"I'm not a chicken. I'm a *gurr*," said Clary indignantly. She climbed up onto a stool and poured the whole bag of sugar into a bowl.

Maisie poured most of it back. Between the three of them they somehow got the cake into the oven. Clary licked the beaters, and Maisie washed the icing from her face. Then they went over to the church to dust the pews. Clary was more thorough than Maisie, intently polishing every inch.

Babysitting was going to be just as easy as last summer. Maisie could get her usual morning chores done, and Clary was easy to be with—so long as she got her own way. She seemed to like Maisie now, as she solemnly told her about Mickey. He was helping Clary dust.

"You missed a spot, Mickey," she scolded. She looked up. "He's *so* smaw he can't hardwy hode the duster. Can you make him a smawer piece?"

Maisie bit the rag and tore off a corner. Clary grinned with approval as she handed it to Mickey.

When they had finished dusting, they went back to the kitchen and had tea and warm cake with Granny. Clary drank out of a tiny cup that used to be Maisie's. Granny poured a drop of tea into it, filled up the rest with milk, and added lots of honey: she called it "cambric tea."

"Sing 'ever seen a wassie'!" Clary ordered Granny.

"Not until you say the magic word," Maisie reminded her.

"*Pwease.*"

"'Did you ever see a lassie / Go this way and that way?'" sang Granny, waving one arm, then another.

Clary copied her. By the end of the song Maisie and Granny were dancing her around the kitchen, swinging her out to each side. "'Go *this* way and *that* way / Go *this* way and *that* way!'" they shouted, as Clary shrieked with joy. They collapsed in giggles and had some water.

Maisie took Clary to the privy and walked her

back to her house. She enjoyed these small, satisfying tasks of looking after a child: washing her hands, putting on her hat, helping her down the stairs. It was so much easier than the huge responsibility of looking after her parents.

ॐ

For the next few days Maisie sank gratefully into the familiar rhythms of summer. Every morning she and Clary helped Granny bake or clean or weed or make cigarettes out of tobacco and paper. Clary was entranced with Granny's new machine, which rolled out five cigarettes at once.

When Clary got bored, they went down to the beach and dug in the sand and paddled. Maisie constructed a tiny sailboat for Mickey out of driftwood and a leaf. Precisely at noon she would deliver Clary to her parents and walk back to the rectory.

Right after lunch Una arrived. Then they went to one of their usual haunts. Maisie relished revisiting each one: walking to the lighthouse, rowing out to the little island they called "the Boot," and hiking up Vulture Ridge. They whizzed along the dusty road on their bikes, passing fields of cows and sheep. Each afternoon ended with a swim.

In other summers Susan or Doris or Wendy would

sometimes join them on their excursions, but so far Maisie had Una all to herself. To her relief her cousin wore her usual shorts and T-shirt instead of her fancy outfits. The lipstick didn't appear again. If it wasn't for her hair, she would look the same.

The only problem was that Una was so dreamy and distracted she seemed half-asleep. "I've asked you twice what you want to do today, and you haven't answered!" complained Maisie. "What are you thinking about all the time?"

Una flushed. "Sorry, George. Let's go to the light-house and watch for whales."

She hadn't answered the question, but Maisie let it go. She didn't want to disturb the equilibrium that was between them these days.

Except for the weekends, their families ate separately. But after dinner each night Maisie and Una would meet in their special place: an old shack that Polly and her childhood friends had fixed up years before, in the woods behind the church.

Maisie and Una called it "the Hut." They often slept on the old mattress, talking long into the night. Every day they tidied, sweeping the wood floor and carefully pinning back the canvas curtains. They brought flowers in a vase to place on the table made of boxes, and old cushions to soften the stump chairs.

The Hut was a museum of their childhood. Their

old dolls and stuffed animals had been banished to a corner. A cowboy hat and a mask were hung on top of Maisie's holster and pistol, from the summer they pretended they were the Lone Ranger and Tonto.

On the walls were pinned descriptions of the cases the girls had solved when they were Nancy Drew and her best chum, George. They had played this game from ages nine to twelve. Maisie had insisted that Una be Nancy, despite Una's protests that Maisie was better at solving mysteries. But in the books Nancy was perfect: brave and clever, as she dashed around in her blue roadster and helped everyone. Maisie wanted all that for Una. She was perfectly content being the awkward, boyish friend.

Two summers ago, however, Una had declared that they were far too old to play such a childish game. She was right, of course; but Maisie mourned the game's intensity and closeness. At least they had kept their secret names.

After that they spent most of their time in the Hut playing cards and Monopoly or sprawled on the mattress with their books. Maisie was addicted to Agatha Christie mysteries. Una liked trashy romances, which she kept on reading despite Maisie's scorn.

This summer Una had dragged out an old windup gramophone. She played "Be My Love" again and again.

"Can't we listen to something else?" Maisie complained.

"But didn't you see *The Great Caruso*? I loved it!"

"Nope. Remember, we only have one movie theatre in Duncan."

"I saw it three times! Mario Lanza is my absolute favourite movie star. Who's yours?"

"Katharine Hepburn. Did you see her in *Adam's Rib*? She was a lawyer—like your mum!"

"But who's your favourite male actor?"

Maisie shrugged. "I don't have one."

"Well, you can share Mario Lanza with me. I wish you could see all the movies I do, George."

Una went to a different matinee every Saturday with her new classmates. She talked about these friends incessantly: Elin, Penny, Karen, and especially a girl called Bev.

"There's something I've been meaning to tell you, George," said Una on Thursday evening. Her face looked especially twitchy.

"What?" Was Una about to divulge another secret?

"I've—well, I've asked Bev to stay for a week. She's arriving on Sunday evening."

"*This* Sunday? But why didn't you say anything?"

"Well . . . I just heard from her."

Una paused, and Maisie realized she was seeking approval. She took a deep breath to calm her panic.

"Why not?" she made herself answer. "I'd like to meet her."

She didn't, of course—she didn't want to share Una with anyone! *She* had never asked a friend from school to stay, so why would Una? This was the first summer Una had friends off the island . . . but couldn't she just see them in the city?

Una looked relieved. "Great! Bev is so much fun. She knows a lot about fashion. She told me that my clothes were too young, so last month Mum gave me some money and Bev took me shopping for new ones."

Maisie already disliked Bev. And she was arriving in only three days! Now Maisie felt desperate to fit as much of Una as possible into that time. "Do you want to sleep here tonight?" she asked.

"Sure! I'll get my stuff."

Granny and Grand were sitting on the veranda, watching the sunset. "We're going to sleep in the Hut tonight," Maisie told them.

"It's a beautiful, warm night for it," said Grand. "Look at that colour, Maisie! The Old Man is really at his paintbox tonight." That was Grand's nickname for God.

"Don't forget to brush your teeth," said Granny. "I'll wake you up so you're in time for Clary."

They looked so peaceful, side by side in the swinging chair. Granny was knitting, of course—she never had what she called "idle fingers." Grand had the newspaper, but it was lying across his knees as he gazed at the sky.

Before, Mum and Dad used to sit in front of the fire like this, quietly chatting about the day's events. Maisie would snuggle into Dad's lap while he told her a fairy tale. Mum would laugh as he changed the words to "Little Red Walking Hood" or "Snow White and the Seven Rats."

Don't think of that! Maisie kissed her grandparents goodnight, got her things, and went back to the Hut.

"Mum will be here tomorrow," said Una, as they lay in bed. Remember not to say that I told you about my father."

"Of course I won't! Your secret is safe with me," Maisie assured her. They chatted lazily, then fell asleep to the sound of the waves.

☙

The next evening they met Maud at the wharf.

"Maisie!" she cried, after she'd kissed Una. Her hug was so strong that Maisie gasped.

Maud let her go and gazed at her fondly. Maisie grinned back. She had always felt more comfortable with Maud than with any of the other adults, even Polly.

Grand had once said that Maud was like a ship in full sail. She strode proudly with long steps, her generous bosom leading the way. Except for her hair, Una didn't look at all like her. Maud's long face had a beaked nose like an eagle's, and her brown eyes were sharp and curious. She wore her thick hair very short, and permed it so it fell back from her broad forehead in waves. As usual, she was dressed stylishly, in a navy-blue linen suit, red beads, and red sandals.

Dinner was at Granny and Grand's. Maud regaled them with a story about her latest court case. Her firm was defending a woman who was accused of poisoning her husband.

"I can't reveal the details, of course, but I *know* we're going to win. I've discovered something that's going to destroy their whole case."

"You tell 'em, Boss," said her father proudly.

"Oh, Maud, I just can't believe you're involved in such sordid things!" said Granny.

"You didn't think I would ever be a lawyer—but I am!" crowed Maud.

After dinner they sat in the living room and devoured most of the huge box of cherries Maud had brought over.

"Don't eat too many—I want to preserve them," protested Granny.

But the sweet cherries were addictive; Maisie couldn't stop grabbing more handfuls. Clary's mouth was rimmed with red, and juice dribbled down her front. When Maisie and Una showed her how to make cherry earrings, Clary insisted that they all wear some. Even Grand draped a pair around his ears.

♨

On Saturday Maud, Una, and Maisie rowed to the Boot for a picnic. For the first time, Maisie beat Maud in a race around the island.

"I hereby bequeath to you the title of Best Swimmer in the Family," said Maud, pulling herself up and gasping. They collapsed on the warm sandstone and gobbled their lunch.

"Can you bear to tell me about your father?" Maud asked. Her voice was unusually gentle.

Not again! "He's just the same," muttered Maisie.

"Poor Gregor." Maud sighed. "Even after all these years I can't believe that my teasing cousin has become so sad. And now he sounds desperate. Is he getting any help?"

"He's going to a doctor."

"What kind of doctor?"

Maisie shrugged. "Just our family one—Dr. Mc-Callum."

Maud looked firm. "It sounds like he needs a psychiatrist. I'll telephone Sadie about it—maybe

Gregor could come and stay at my place and see someone in Vancouver."

"A psychiatrist! But that's for crazy people! Dad
isn't c-crazy!"

"*Crazy* isn't a very helpful word, Maisie. Your dad
is obviously deeply troubled. There's nothing shameful about it. Lots of men were affected badly by the
war. He should have seen someone long ago, before
he broke down. A good psychiatrist could help him."

"Maybe. But I know he won't see one. He won't
do *anything*!" Maisie added angrily.

"We'll see." Maud smoothed out the wax paper
from her sandwich. "Now, I don't want *you* to worry
about this. Your dad is having a very difficult time, but
all of us are going to help him get through it. Leave
it to the adults, though—none of this is *your* concern.
Your job is to have as good a time as you can this
summer—okay?"

Maisie couldn't help returning her grin. Maud
always made her feel as if she could fix anything. A
small flame of hope ignited in her—maybe Maud
could fix Dad, as well.

The sea glittered around them as they stretched
out in the sun. Maisie closed her eyes and listened to
the squawk of a heron.

Please, God, may Dad get better, she prayed.

CHAPTER SIX

Bev

Una waved to a skinny girl in high heels who was tottering down the gangplank behind Aunt Esther. "There she is! Bev, Bev!"

Bev wore a flouncy green dress, sunglasses with glitter on them, and a green print kerchief tied under her chin.

"Does the lass think she's Princess Elizabeth?" whispered Granny.

Una introduced Maisie to her friend. Bev dismissed her with one glance. "My *God*, Una, the boat rolled so much I thought I'd be sick! And I sat on something and stained my new dress—do you think it will come out?"

Granny poked Maisie, who went up to Aunt Esther and hugged her. Then she murmured, "I'm so sorry about your brother."

"So am I, Esther, dear," said Granny. "And we're sorry we couldn't get to the funeral, but I needed to be here for Maisie."

"Thank you," said Aunt Esther. "Ben was much too young to leave us."

She looked older and greyer, and her eyes were stricken. Uncle Daniel put his arm around her and led her away.

"Una! You have to help me with my bags!"

Bev's suitcase was so heavy that Una and Maisie had to lift it together. What did she have in here?

Maud put her hand on Maisie's shoulder. "Have a *great* week," she said dryly. She was leaving on the same boat.

"Goodbye, Mrs. Brown," called Bev.

Why did she call Maud "Mrs."? Then Maisie remembered.

Maisie and Una had to carry the heavy suitcase all the way to Una's house.

Bev stumbled beside them with her purse and shoulder bag. "I'm going to lose a heel on this rough road!" she complained.

"Take your shoes off, then," said Maisie.

"Are you kidding? And walk in my stocking feet? I hope all your roads aren't like this."

"I'm afraid they are," said Una anxiously. "Didn't you bring any other shoes?"

"Sandals. I'll just have to wear them all the time I'm here, even though they don't go with everything."

❧

As the week wore on, Maisie almost took pleasure in hating Bev. It was like rolling in mud and getting so dirty she didn't care.

How could Una possibly like this mewling creature? Bev changed into a new stylish outfit every day. She was so puny she couldn't even lift a pail of water. She couldn't believe they didn't have electricity and was insulted that she had to use a privy instead of an indoor toilet.

Bev acted afraid of everything—a mouse in a trap, the bats at night—but Maisie didn't think she was truly afraid of a thing. She seemed too hard and calculating.

Una's grandmother had given Una a week off hotel work. She and Bev slept in every morning and then just hung around on the veranda, reading movie magazines and giggling. Maisie tried to keep Clary away from them. The mornings with Granny or on the beach or walking to the store were soothing breaks from Bev's shrill, whiny voice.

When Maisie returned Clary, however, she had to encounter Bev again.

Clary disliked her, as well. "Your knees are *bony*," she complained the first morning, as Bev tried to read her a story. "I want to get down."

Bev just clutched her tighter.

"Don't!" Clary pinched Bev's arm and stomped off to her father in the kitchen.

"Oh, Bev, I'm so sorry," said Una.

"I'm going to have a bruise!" said Bev, rubbing her arm. "What a brat!"

"She's not!" said Maisie. "She's just being two, that's all. You should have let her down when she asked."

"She should be punished!" said Bev.

Maisie opened her mouth to retort but stopped when she saw her cousin's worried face. Una acted so afraid of her friend, so eager to get her approval. That made Maisie hate Bev even more.

Chester appeared with a plate of sandwiches. "Want to stay for lunch, Maisie?"

She shook her head and fled home.

But Maisie couldn't think of an excuse not to join in the excursions they went on every afternoon. Una seemed desperate to find an activity that Bev liked. On the first few days they took her hiking, rode their bikes to Shell Bay, and canoed to the Boot. Bev said she hated boats, and she wobbled on her bike. The hike made her too sweaty, and the shelly sand scratched her legs.

Finally they just did what Bev wanted: they sat

on the veranda sipping lemonade, sat in the Hut and talked, or sat on the beach and tanned.

Bev tried the water on her first day, stuffing her hair into a white rubber bathing cap. "It's *freezing*!" she shrieked. She never went in again but lolled on her towel, unclipping the straps of her bathing suit and encouraging Una to do the same. Maisie watched Una struggle to keep her top from falling down, but she didn't feel sorry for her. Why did she have to copy everything Bev did?

Una and Bev talked incessantly about school, about every girl in their class and every teacher. The worst was when Bev would whisper something to Una that made her giggle. They had a secret! A secret that excluded Maisie. She had never felt so invisible or alone.

"What are those papers on the wall?" asked Bev the first time they went to the Hut.

Una flushed. "Oh, just a silly game that Maisie and I played when we were kids. We should take them down." Una got up and unpinned all the papers and maps about Nancy and George.

"It *wasn't* silly!" Maisie snatched the papers from her and smoothed them out. "It was really fun. We used to get up early and spy on people through their windows. Then we'd make notes about any suspicious activities we saw."

"You peeked through people's windows? That's so

nosy!" Bev paused, then asked, "Did you ever see anything . . . you know . . . *private*?"

Una glanced at Maisie. "No! And you're right, Bev—it *was* nosy. But we were very young then."

Maisie smirked. She was glad Una hadn't said anything about the time they had crept up to Mr. and Mrs. Lewis's bedroom window and saw them entwined and giggling. The girls had been so shocked that they'd scurried away.

The next time they were at the Hut, Bev put down her magazine and yawned. "I'm bored. There's nothing to do on this island."

"Una and I are *never* bored here," said Maisie coldly. She paused. "We used to play buried treasure—do you remember, Una? We'd bury something like a painted shell or some costume jewellery and then make a map of where to find it. Then we'd leave the map around the store or the wharf and wait for someone to pick it up. But only one person ever did, that summer visitor who—"

"*Maisie*, don't be ridiculous—we haven't played that stupid game for years!"

We did it last summer, thought Maisie. But Una's scoffing tone was so hurtful she turned silent.

"I have a great idea," said Bev. She took out a piece of newspaper from her pocket. "I tore this out on the boat. It's a want ad—from a sailor!"

"What do you mean?" asked Una.

Bev read aloud: "'Lonely sailor stationed in Vancouver would like to correspond with attractive woman aged 20–25. Tell me all about yourself and maybe we can get together.'"

Maisie snatched the ad from Bev and read it herself in case Bev was lying. But sure enough, those were the exact words. How strange and pathetic, to advertise for someone in a newspaper!

Bev glared at Maisie. "Give that back, please."

Maisie handed the ad over. "So what's your great idea?" she said scornfully.

"So I thought we could write him back!" said Bev. "We could pretend to be a woman he'd want to meet."

"Let's!" said Una, but her voice quivered.

Maisie watched the two of them bend over a piece of paper and compose the silliest letter she'd ever heard. It was full of phrases like "I have beautiful brunette hair and alluring green eyes. I like to dance until dawn, and my lips are as sweet as strawberries." They signed it "Violet Crosby."

Yuck! Maisie retreated to a corner and hid behind her comic. There was a long discussion about which return address to use.

"It can't be mine," said Bev. "My mother is really strict. She'd have a fit if I got a letter from a stranger. We can use your address on the island, Una."

"That's not fair!" said Maisie. "What if *Una's* mother

asks her about it? Why should she get into trouble and not you?"

"Oh, don't be so paranoid. She can just say it's a letter from me. Shall I write down your address, Una?"

"I suppose so," said Una. "He won't answer anyway."

"How can he resist?" Bev giggled. "It's such an alluring letter he won't be able to help it!"

Una found an envelope. "I'm not going to put my address on the outside—the postmistress looks at everything." She addressed it and said she'd sneak it into the mail later.

"Let's do it now, before you forget," said Bev. The two of them walked away, their heads together as they giggled over the envelope.

Maisie wanted to scream like Clary. She was losing her best friend! Losing her to this . . . *cretin*, this stupid idiot who had roped Una into her ridiculous scheme. What if the sailor answered? Una would be in terrible trouble, and Bev would get away scot-free.

It was as if Bev had cast a spell over Una . . . and there was nothing Maisie could do to save her.

એ

The weather became hotter and hotter. "It was eighty-six at the Vancouver airport yesterday," said Grand on Friday, looking up from the newspaper.

"It's going to be just as hot today," said Granny. "And we've been a month without rain! What will we do if we run out of garden water?" Granny collected rainwater in barrels.

"Don't worry, my dear," said Grand. "This drought can't last much longer."

"Oh, look, Maisie!" Granny passed over her section of the paper. "It's a photograph of Charles and Anne! The 'royal toddlers,' they call them. Aren't they the sweetest children you've ever seen? I must cut this out for my scrapbook."

"They don't look any different than other kids," growled Maisie. "Clary is just as cute."

Granny examined her. "Well, *someone* got out of bed on the wrong side this morning! It must be the heat that's making you so cranky. You three girls had better sleep in your cabin tonight—it will be much cooler. Do you have enough beds out there?"

"There's only the mattress, but Una and Bev can have it," muttered Maisie. "I'll stay in Mum and Dad's room." She had slept there last night—it was much cooler than the attic.

"But you'll want to be with your friends," said Granny.

When Maisie didn't answer, Granny patted her arm. "You've never had to share Una before, have you, chickie? Never mind, Bev's leaving on Sunday. I must say, I've never met such a stroppy lass."

"Now, Jean . . ."

Granny kissed Grand's forehead. "I know—I should be more charitable. But you have to agree, Rand, that Bev is much too fancy for the island." She turned to Maisie. "All the same, she's Una's guest, so you have to be polite. I think you should join them in the Hut. Polly and Chester have an extra cot."

Maisie had no choice but to agree. Bev, of course, pretended to be nervous about sleeping outside. Chester hauled out a cot, and Bev had to have extra blankets because "I get cold so easily."

Finally they were snuggled in bed. At least Bev was in the cot. Maisie felt soothed, curled up beside her cousin as usual. They had shared this lumpy old mattress since they were six, the first time they'd been allowed to sleep here. When they were children, they'd clung together like spoons. Maisie wished she could still burrow against Una's back; she'd always had a faintly tangy smell, like lemon or ginger. But they were teenagers now, too old to snuggle together like little kids.

There was a scuttling noise outside. "What's *that*?" asked Bev.

"Probably just a raccoon," Maisie told her.

"Can it get in?"

"It *could* climb in the window," she said.

"Don't be silly, Maisie," said Una. "It won't climb in, Bev—don't worry."

"Why don't we tell ghost stories," suggested Maisie. "I know a great one called 'Bloody Fingers.'"

Bev gave her little fake scream. "No! You'll give me nightmares!"

She and Una began to talk about a girl at school named Hilda. "She's too fat, and she laughs too much," pronounced Bev.

"But I *like* Hilda," said Una.

"You'd better not," warned Bev. "Nobody else does."

If that's what Bev thought about poor Hilda, what did she think about *her*? wondered Maisie. But she already knew that their hatred was mutual.

She lay very still and pretended to sleep, straining to hear their whispers. At first they talked about a prefect named Pippa, how lenient she was.

Then Bev said urgently, "I'm sure she's asleep. Tell me again what he said."

Una answered, her voice so whispery that Maisie could barely make out her words. She heard "coming soon" and "his mother" and, louder, "He said he's really looking forward to seeing me again!"

"Oh, Una, how romantic!" said Bev.

Maisie sat bolt upright. "Who are you talking about? *Who's* coming?"

Now they were all sitting up. Bev looked at Maisie with such smug pity that Maisie wanted to slap her.

She turned to Una. "*Who's* coming?" she repeated.

"Oh, Maisie," said Una. "It's just . . . David."

"David! You mean David Meyer?"

"Yes—Bubby's nephew. Remember I told you how I met him at the funeral? Bubby has asked his mother to visit, and David's coming, too."

"When?"

"At the end of the month, for two weeks."

"He wrote Una and told her. He's coming to see *her!*" said Bev triumphantly.

"Well, he didn't *exactly* say that," muttered Una.

"You've been writing to David?" Maisie asked.

"Yes!" said Bev. "And *he's* written twice! Una has a huge crush on him!"

"Please, Bev . . . that's just between you and me."

Maisie was so hurt she could hardly get out her words. "W-Why didn't you *tell* me you've been writing to David?"

"I'm so sorry, Maise." Una's voice was stricken. "Let's talk about this another time, okay?"

She plunked down, turned her back, and was silent. Maisie and Bev had no choice but to do the same.

Maisie listened to the two of them breathe softly. But she tossed in agony, trying to get her mind around what Bev had said.

&

For the next two days Maisie avoided the other two girls. She slept in the rectory on Saturday night and spent her time in the backyard workshop, measuring and cutting wood for a bookcase she was going to make for Granny. Grand had never been good at carpentry, but this was where Dad kept the tools he'd had since he was a boy. Every summer he and Maisie would work on a project. One year they'd constructed ten purple martin houses and given some away to the neighbours. Last summer they made a new table for the parish hall. Dad had been as silent and irritable as usual, but at least he'd *done* something.

Would he this summer? *Probably not*, thought Maisie bitterly. He would just sit around, the way he did at home.

Finally Bev left on the Sunday evening boat. Maisie avoided talking to Una at the family dinner that night, but after they did the dishes Una suggested going for a walk.

"I—I guess I should tell you about David," gulped Una, as they trudged towards the wharf. The doe with the twins bounded ahead of them. Already the fawns were bigger and bolder. One turned around and stared before it joined the others.

"You don't have to tell me," said Maisie. "Let's just forget it."

"No . . . I *want* to tell you."

They sat on the coronation seat, facing each other. Una's tan made the green in her eyes more vivid. In the summer she turned as "brown as a berry," as Granny said. Maisie only got more freckled.

"I'm sorry Bev was a pain," said Una. "She's much easier to get along with in the city."

"I just don't understand how you can like her! Are all your new friends like that?"

"No. But Bev . . . well, she's one of the most popular girls in our class. I guess I was just flattered that she wanted to visit. I'm sorry you had to put up with her."

Maisie shrugged. "She's gone now. Let's just forget about her."

"I'll explain about David now."

Una began talking, and Maisie stared at the sea, hating every word. How friendly David had been at the funeral, how he'd written to thank her for spending so much time with him. "He said I was the only person there he could really talk to," said Una solemnly. She had written back and David had responded, saying he was coming to visit the island.

"Aunt Esther invited him along with his mother," said Maisie. "He's not coming to see *you*," she added meanly.

"I think he is!" said Una fervently. "In his letters

84

David asked me all sorts of questions—he seems really interested in me."

Maisie could barely form her words. "But Una, David is *twenty*!"

"So what? I'll be fifteen at the end of the month. That's only five years younger. And of course we're just friends, so far . . . but oh, Maisie, I like him so much! He's the kindest and handsomest and most intelligent boy I've ever met. It's such a relief to be able to tell you."

"But why didn't you before?"

"Well . . . because when I arrived, you were so upset at how I looked. It seems to bother you that I'm acting like a teenager. You're *such* a tomboy, George," she said fondly. "You're just not interested in boys yet. Bubby says you will be one day, that we're growing up at different rates. So I didn't want to upset you again. But now you know, and I'm so glad you do. Wait till you see David again, Maisie. He's completely different from the way he used to be, not at all standoffish. You'll like him just as much as I do."

No, I won't! thought Maisie. Una continued to babble obsessively. No wonder she was so distracted this summer. David was all she could think of.

Neither of them said the words, but they hung in the air as truthfully as the deep sea around them. Una didn't just *like* David. She was falling in love with him.

CHAPTER SEVEN

Waiting for David

Granny was excited about the coming visitors. "They both need a good rest," she said. "That dear boy, losing his father at such a young age. And poor Rachel—how will she cope?"

"Daniel says that Ben provided well for her," said Grand. "She'll have the house and a good income."

Granny looked stricken. "I couldn't *bear* to live my life without you, Rand!"

Grand got up and kissed her forehead. "Now, now, that's a very long time in the future."

Maisie was reading a letter from Mum.

"Any news?" asked Granny brightly.

She meant, was there any news about Dad.

Maisie handed her the short letter: a bland account of Mrs. Hanna's terrible cat, the opening of the new hardware store, and how hot it was—as if the weather were different from here! "Dad sends his love" was her usual ending. That meant nothing had changed. As Granny read the letter, Maisie could see how disappointed she was.

"Well, it won't be long before we'll have them here," she said.

Maisie didn't want to think of that. And it *was* long, over a month.

"Listen, Rand!" Granny waved part of the paper at him. "It says that *Brigadoon* is coming to Vancouver! I've always longed to see that."

"Mmm," said Grand behind his section.

"Did you know, chickie, that on August 7 your grandfather and I will have been married for forty-two years?"

Grand winked at Maisie. "My dear Jean . . . would you like me to take you to see *Brigadoon* for our anniversary?"

Granny beamed. "Oh, Rand, what a good idea!"

❧

For the next blissful two weeks Maisie had Una completely to herself. Each day dawned clear and cloudless. The adults began to count the number of days since the drought had begun—forty-seven, fifty . . .

Every Sunday they prayed for rain, and the girls were reminded constantly not to use too much water.

Maisie stopped taking her outdoor shower under the cistern. She plunged into the sea before breakfast and cooled off in it many more times during the day. Her hair and skin became frosted with salt. So did her clothes, which she rinsed out in the sea instead of giving to Granny to wash. Her underwear scratched, and her shorts and T-shirts became stiff and grey. She didn't care. Instead she relished the feeling of having sea salt next to her skin, as if she were still in the water.

She asked Una not to talk about David to her.

"Sure, if that's what you want," said Una.

She seemed relieved—as if she were just as afraid of his coming as Maisie was. They relaxed into being Nancy and George again.

Maisie neglected her garden chores and forgot to work on her bookcase. Every afternoon they took off somewhere on their bikes, sometimes with one of the island girls but more often alone. Someone had built a raft at Fowler Bay, and they often ended up there, changing into their bathing suits in the bushes and swimming out to it. They would ride home in their wet suits, so much dust glued to their damp skin that they'd need to have another swim when they got home.

Every night they slept in the Hut. The heavy topics—David, their fathers—stayed under the surface, and their chatter was lazy and easy. They lay awake and compared teachers or laughed about Clary's funny comments.

"One of Polly's patrons asked her how old she was," said Una. "Clary said 'Two! I'm quite new.'"

"Granny worries that Clary is spoiled," said Maisie.

"She is! She has Polly and Chester completely under her thumb. She refuses to eat anything but cheese and bread, and they let her! Otherwise she just screams."

"You were like that," said Maisie. "For years you only liked chicken and potatoes, remember? And they couldn't touch each other on the plate! Your mum wouldn't let you have dessert until you'd had at least three mouthfuls of vegetables."

"At least she made me. And I *do* eat vegetables now—some of them, anyway. This year Mum and I went to a restaurant in Seattle where they *only* served vegetables. They cooked them with so many sauces they were delicious!"

Maud sometimes went to Seattle for conferences, and now that Una was living with her full-time she took her along. When Una talked about visiting there or going to the symphony or a play, Maisie realized how much her cousin's world had expanded since she'd gone to live in the city.

"We're going to Toronto for Thanksgiving," she

told Maisie. "Mum's taking a week off. We're staying at Aunt Sylvia's, and I get to miss school. We're flying on an airplane!"

"You're so lucky!" Maisie told her. "I've never been *anywhere*." But there was no point in feeling sorry for herself. "Who's Aunt Sylvia?" she asked.

"You know . . . she went to school with our mothers. She's a professor at the University of Toronto. Sometimes she has meetings at U.B.C., and then she stays with us."

Maisie remembered now—her mother and Maud and Sylvia and three other girls had shared a dorm at boarding school in Victoria. Maud had often told Maisie what a clown her mother was then. But now Dad's sadness had sucked all the fun out of her.

༄

One afternoon while Clary was napping the girls visited Polly's studio. The walls were hung with her newest paintings—bright fuzzy stripes of brown, orange, yellow, and green. When Maisie squinted, she realized they were arbutus trees.

"What do you think?" asked Polly.

"They're wonderful! I like how there are other colours under the top colours, like . . ." She couldn't think of the word.

"*Layers* . . . that's what's so great about watercolours—they're so transparent. I was trying to layer the brown bark and the peeling red bark and the green under that."

Maisie couldn't stop staring at the paintings. Somehow Polly had captured the essence of the island in them, its freshness and light. How talented she was!

"I think these are your best work," said Una.

"Thank you! I'm really excited about them. By the end of the summer I should have enough for a show. It's going to be in Edmonton this time. That's where Biddy lives."

"Who's Biddy?" asked Maisie.

"She used to be my best friend on the island. But her family moved to the prairies when we were teenagers. Over the years we've stopped writing, but I'm hoping to see her at the opening." Polly sighed. "When you have a family and a career, it's hard to keep in touch. I had another close friend, Eleanor, but she moved to England. We only write at Christmas."

"Maisie and I will *always* be friends," said Una. She grabbed Maisie's hand and kissed it.

Maisie felt the warmth of the kiss on the back of her hand for the rest of the day.

One evening Maisie couldn't sleep. "Nance? Are you awake?" she whispered.

"I am now," grumbled Una.

"Let's go skinny-dipping!" It took a few minutes for Maisie to persuade Una to leave the cozy bed, but finally she agreed. They gathered up towels and flashlights and headed down to the beach.

A half moon hung in the sky. Maisie bounced her light from the road to the rectory to the treetops. She felt eleven again, sneaking out in the magical night with her partner in crime.

When they reached the shore, Maisie cried, "Look—luminescence!" Radiant waves lapped on the sand, breaking into flashes of light.

After stripping off their pyjamas, they ventured into the icy sea. They splashed it into fiery explosions, drawing sparkling circles and dribbling shining water over their bodies.

Maisie was the first to duck. She gasped at the coldness, but there was nothing in the world so satisfying as feeling the silky sea against her skin. She swam and rolled and dived, feeling as much a part of the water as did a fish or an otter or a seal.

Una bobbed beside her as they lay on their backs and looked at the stars. Then they swam to shore, blazing a trail behind them.

They stood on the sand, rubbing down their

shivering bodies. "I *wish* I wasn't so fat," moaned Maisie, looking down at her blobby tummy.

"You're not fat—you're just right!" said Una.

Maisie knew she was lying to make her feel better—but it worked. She watched Una as she towelled her hair. *Her* body was perfect, so smooth and firm, with small apple breasts. Maisie could have stared at her forever; but Una put on her pyjamas, and they hurried back to bed to get warm.

§

On July 29 Uncle Daniel and Aunt Esther asked the whole family to a party for Una's fifteenth birthday. The hotel chef made her a huge cake, decorated with piped yellow roses and fifteen candles. Clary helped Una blow them out. Maisie wondered what she had wished for. Probably something about David, she decided.

Una passed around pieces of cake, her face shining with content. Tonight she was all dressed up in one of her fancy dresses. Maud had let her wear lipstick. Her perm was growing out, and it looked more natural, curling only at the ends.

Maisie had made Una a small cedar box; it had taken her two whole days to construct. She had glowed at Una's effusive thanks, even though she said she'd keep her makeup in it.

It was far too hot to wear a wool kilt. Instead Granny had found a dress for Maisie in the church donation box. It wasn't too bad: a simple green cotton shift that felt loose and cool. Granny had also made Maisie have a shower and wash her hair. It fluffed around her face and felt light and airy.

"How pretty you look tonight, Maisie!" Uncle Daniel smiled at her. "You and Una are growing up so fast, the way my girls did. It seems just yesterday that I carried Polly around like this little one." Clary was on his shoulders, eating cake and dropping crumbs into his hair.

"Who's Pawy?" demanded Clary.

He chuckled. "Polly is your mother!"

"No, she isn't. *My* mother is Mummy!"

"I've made up the best rooms, the two facing the water," Aunt Esther was telling Maud. "A family from Victoria wanted them, but I said I was saving them for my relatives. So we've lost some customers, but I don't care."

She was talking about David and his mother. They were arriving tomorrow! All day Maisie had managed to shove that fact out of her head, but now it loomed over her.

"Are we still sleeping in the Hut tonight?" she asked Una desperately.

"Of course!"

෫ඁ

Once they were in bed, Una was unusually silent. *She's thinking about David,* thought Maisie bitterly. She began chattering about the party, just to keep Una awake. Everything was going to change tomorrow—she just knew it! This would be the last night that was the same.

"Wasn't Clary funny when she ordered us to relight the candles so she could blow them out again?" said Maisie.

Una barely responded. But then she said slowly, "Maise . . . have you ever kissed a boy?"

Maisie cleared her throat. "Well, um . . . yes, I have."

Now Una sat up. "You *have*? What was it like? Tell me *everything*!"

So Maisie did, as every detail about that long day rushed back.

Mum had bought her a pale-yellow dress for the grade nine graduation dance. It was the plainest one she could find, and Maisie was resigned to wearing it for just two occasions. The dance was held in the school gym in the afternoon. That evening one of the girls was having a party at her house.

Jim walked her to the school. She felt so easy with him that she was almost looking forward to the event. As at previous dances, she and Jim could hang around the food table and just watch everyone.

As soon as they entered the gym, however, and Maisie saw all the couples gyrating to "Come On-a My House," her nose started to bleed. Blood sloshed over the yellow dress and all over her hands as she tried to stop the flow.

Jim took her to the nurse's office. Maisie spent an hour there, lying on her back with a cold washcloth over her face. The nurse told her to pinch her nostrils until the bleeding stopped. When it finally did, she walked home in her blood-splattered dress, people giving her incredulous glances as she passed them.

"Oh, *pickle* . . ." cried Mum in despair at her bloodied state. "What am I to do with you?" She whisked off the dress, put it in the sink, and told Maisie to have a bath. Miraculously, all the blood came out. Maisie put on the clean, freshly ironed dress, and Jim picked her up for the party.

Maisie was terrified that her nose would bleed again, but it was fine. And so was the party. At first everyone jitterbugged. Maisie wasn't very good at that, but neither was Jim. Then they just sat around and drank Coke and gorged on chips and talked about how wonderful it was to be done with school. Maisie made a big joke out of her nosebleed. It was the first time she had felt relaxed at a mixed party.

Jim walked her home. It was a warm, fragrant night, and the smell of roses surrounded them as they stood at Maisie's front door.

"Would you—would you mind if I kissed you?" murmured Jim.

Maisie was so surprised that all she could answer was "I guess not."

Jim bent towards her. His lips pressed against hers for a few seconds. Maisie drew back, but Jim kissed her again. This time he lingered longer.

"That's enough!" said Maisie, pushing him away.

Jim looked angry. "What's the matter with you, Maisie—it's just a kiss!" He stomped down the street.

"You pushed him away?" said Una. "But why?"

"Because . . . because I didn't *like* it!" Maisie's voice quivered. "I know your first kiss is supposed to be earth-shattering and wonderful—but it was *nothing*! Just like Granny or Grand kissing me. But everyone makes such a fuss about it! Is Jim right? *Is* there something the matter with me?"

"There's *nothing* the matter with you, Maisie! Jim must have been the wrong boy, that's all. You don't have . . . *feelings* about him, right?"

"Right! He's just a friend. He *was*, anyway," she added sadly.

"Then don't worry about it. When you meet the *right* boy, you'll enjoy kissing him, I'm sure."

Then Maisie confessed her greatest worry. "You know what? I don't think I will . . . no matter who the boy is. I'm just not interested! And I don't ever want to have sex, either. Do you think I have to?"

Una chuckled. "You're so funny, George. Of course you don't *have* to, but when you get married, I bet you'll *want* to." She looked nervous. "Sex *does* seem scary and kind of . . . weird. But doing it is an expression of how much you love your husband—that's what Mum says."

"But maybe I won't get married," said Maisie. "Then I won't have to have sex!"

Now Una sounded exasperated. "It's way too soon to decide that. It'll be years before you get married."

"*If* I do . . . You know what? I'm just not going to!"

"But don't you want to have children?"

"Maybe . . ."

"You can't have children unless you get married!" crowed Una. "*I'm* going to have four girls—Clara and Esther after my grandmothers, Maud after Mum . . . and the youngest will be called Mairead after you!"

Maisie grinned. "Thanks! I'll leave her my great-grandmother's mirror . . . because if I need to get married to have children, then I guess I won't have anyone else to leave it to."

"Don't be so stubborn, George—*everyone* gets married!"

"Your mum didn't."

"Well . . . she still could someday. Once I asked

her why she wasn't married, and she said she was too busy. But I think she just hasn't met the right man."

"Well, *I'm* not going to!" The decision felt so surprisingly right that Maisie almost laughed out loud.

"You shouldn't decide so soon! You don't know what will happen when you're older. I bet you'll marry a wonderful man, and then the sex and everything will be fine."

Maisie stared at Una. "How do you know? Have *you* ever kissed a boy?"

"Not yet. Bev has, though! A boy on her street asked her to go for a walk, and he kissed her in the park under the full moon. That's so romantic!"

"I do *not* want to talk about stupid Bev!"

"Sure. But oh, Maisie, *please* can't we talk about—"

"I'm going to sleep now," said Maisie abruptly. She rolled over on her side away from Una.

"You are?" Una sounded disappointed. When Maisie didn't answer, she sighed and said, "Night-night, George. And don't worry. I know you'll meet the right boy one day."

"Good night," murmured Maisie.

Una tossed beside her. Maisie knew she was so excited about David's arrival that she couldn't sleep.

Neither could Maisie. She went over and over their conversation. Did she *really* not want to get married and have children? Was Una right? Was the fiasco with Jim simply because he was the wrong boy? All her embarrassment flooded back. When she saw Jim in the fall, they could never be friends again. He'd spoiled everything!

At least Una hadn't yet had her first kiss—but Maisie knew who *she* thought was "the right boy."

CHAPTER EIGHT

Pals

Maisie was determined to hate David as much as she hated Bev. But as soon as she was introduced, his charm overcame her resistance.

"Hello, Maisie," he said softly. "We haven't met for a long time."

David used to be a gangly kid. But now he was the most beautiful boy she'd ever seen. His black hair flopped over his high forehead, and his eyes were dark and intense, edged with thick lashes. He gallantly shook hands with the large number of family members hungrily waiting to greet him.

Una seemed unable to speak. She watched David with a frozen smile on her face, and Maisie watched *her*, noticing how her whole body quivered.

"And here is Maisie!" A small, pale woman shook her hand. "How nice to see you again."

"Hi, Aunt Rachel. I'm sorry about your husband," she added, before Granny had time to prompt her.

"Meet me in the Hut after dinner!" Una whispered.

She was acting so oddly. Maybe she didn't like David after all!

୫ର

"Maisie, I know I promised I wouldn't talk about David, but now that he's here, can't I? *Please?*"

She looked so desperate that of course Maisie let her.

"I don't know what to do!" moaned Una. "He's being so nice, and I can't talk to him! I had lots to say to him at the funeral and in my letters, but now I can't make any words come out! What must he think of me?"

"Who cares what he thinks? He's just a boy," said Maisie. "He seems nice, but you don't have to get so excited about him."

Una started to weep. "He *isn't* just a boy. You don't *understand!*"

Maisie wished that she didn't. She patted Una's shoulder. "Sorry, Nance. I know he means something to you." She paused. "Okay, let's decide what you can do. How about if you begin with little things? Just say 'How was the boat trip,' or something like that. Once you start, I'm sure you'll find it easier. I tell you what—you can practise with me. Pretend I'm David."

Maisie stood up and said in a gruff voice, "Hi, Una."

That made Una chuckle. "Hi, David. Umm—how was the boat trip—was it rough?"

"No, the water was as smooth as glass, and we saw some dolphins. Do you often see them?"

"Sometimes. And we sometimes see whales going down the pass."

"What kind of whales?"

They kept up this inane conversation until they collapsed in giggles. "*Thank you*, Maisie," said Una. "You've made me relax."

"I guess that's the answer when you feel awkward with someone, to just relax," said Maisie. "That's what Granny always says."

"You're right! I know things will go better with David now, especially with your help. What would I do without you, George?"

But Maisie wasn't relaxed at all. How had she, over a few hours, suddenly become the means for Una and David to become closer?

Maisie decided that the only way she could stop a romance developing was to never let the two of them be alone. They were together every morning at the hotel, of course, but surely Una would be so busy cleaning rooms that she wouldn't have a chance to talk to him. David ate lunch at the hotel, and Una ate at home, so there was no danger there.

David had one foot in the adult world and one foot in the teenage one. He sometimes went for walks with his sad mother. But Aunt Rachel spent most of her time with Aunt Esther as they comforted each other in their grief. David fished with Uncle Daniel, or chopped wood for the hotel, or helped guests carry their luggage.

He also seemed to really want to be with Una and Maisie, unlike when they were younger. On many afternoons he turned up after lunch and suggested a swim or a bike ride or a hike. On many evenings he took them out to look at the stars, marvelling at how clear and numerous they were.

"Do you know why they call this time the 'dog days of summer'?" he asked them. "It's because they coincide with Sirius rising. It's the dog star." He pointed out Sirius and many other constellations.

To Maisie's relief, David was equally attentive to both Una and her. He burst with his many enthusiasms: the stars and planets, jazz, art, and faraway countries.

David was shocked by what they hadn't read and made them a long list of his favourite books. Una started on it immediately, but Maisie felt insulted. The list looked too much like school, and anyway, she preferred her cozy mysteries.

Sometimes she found David's passionate monologues overwhelming; he always wanted to *teach* them something, whether the names of the stars or all about the new state of Israel. But everything David told them was so fascinating—far more interesting than anything she'd learned at school—that she couldn't help being intrigued.

"Next summer I'm visiting Europe," David confided. "Dad left me some money, and he always wanted me to travel. This fellow I know at college is coming with me."

Often his eager expression clouded over and he talked about how much he missed his father. Maisie couldn't remember much about Uncle Ben, but Una had seen him a few years ago, when he and Aunt Rachel visited Vancouver.

"He was so much fun!" she told David. "He taught me how to walk on my new stilts and tried them himself."

"He would have liked that, being such a short man," said David, his voice thick with pain.

Una grinned. "He said maybe he should get some himself!"

She was relaxed now. So was Maisie. David seemed interested in Una only in the way he was interested in her, Maisie: as a younger member of the family he could share his grief with and use as a sounding board for his enthusiasms. And the fact that Una never talked to Maisie about him, that she treated him like a friendly older brother, made Maisie sure that her crush was over.

❦

Granny and Grand went to Vancouver for a few days to visit friends and see *Brigadoon*. Maisie and Una were allowed to stay in the rectory by themselves. They made their daytime meals there, then had dinner at Polly's or at the hotel with the rest of the family. In the evenings David walked back with them and they all sat in a row on the veranda. Maisie always made certain she was in the middle.

One evening David lit up a cigarette. "Want one?" he asked them.

"Sure!" said Una.

"Your mother doesn't want you to smoke," pointed out Maisie.

"My mother isn't here," said Una calmly. She held out her cigarette like a movie star and suddenly appeared much older.

"How about you, Maisie?" asked David.

She shook her head. "Granny says I have to wait until I'm twenty-one." Then she squirmed at sounding so prim.

David leaned back and stretched out his long legs to the railing. "Just look at that moon! I bet we'll make it up there one day."

"To the *moon*?" said Una. "That's impossible!"

"I think it *is* possible. All sorts of amazing things are possible—just you wait and see! We're so lucky that the war is over and that we have such a promising future. What are you two going to do?"

"Do when?" asked Una.

"Do when you're grown up, of course. Women can have careers these days—like your mother! You don't just have to get married and be housewives."

"Well, I want to be a pianist, but I don't know if I'm good enough," said Una.

"I think you're excellent!" said David. "I was listening to you play the *Moonlight* Sonata yesterday, and you sounded like a professional!"

"That's a really easy piece," murmured Una, "but thanks."

Her voice was barely audible, but Maisie could tell how thrilled she was.

"How about you, Maisie?" asked David.

Maisie's words spilled out before she knew they

were in her. "What could *I* possibly do! Una is good at piano, and Maud is good at law, and Polly is good at art—but I'm no good at anything! Neither are my parents . . . Mum has never had a job and now my d–dad has given up the ministry. It must run in the family."

Both Una and David whirled to face her.

"Maisie, don't be ridiculous!" said Una. "You're good at everything! You're so strong, and you're an amazing swimmer, and you're so patient with Clary, and you can do carpentry and knit and, and . . . lots of other things!"

"But those are all *little* things! What can I do for a career?"

David looked apologetic. "I'm sorry I asked, Maisie—I didn't mean to put you on the spot. Some people know what they want to do early—I decided to be an astronomer when I was eight. But other people take a long time to find their true calling. Don't worry—you will. And Una's right—you're already good at things. And they *aren't* little—they're important!"

"Thanks." Maisie smiled at David. What a knack he had for making someone feel better!

They gazed at the sparkling sky. "I'll never forget my first time on Kingfisher," said David. "I was only seven, and I'd never realized there were so many stars!"

"Last night when I was babysitting Clary, she wouldn't settle," said Una. "So I wrapped her in a blanket, and we sat on the veranda and looked at the stars. Do you know what she asked me? 'Who put them there?'"

David laughed. "And what did you answer?"

"I just told her God did . . . even though I don't believe that."

"What do you mean?" asked Maisie.

"I mean I don't believe in God."

"*What*? You've never told me that!"

"Well, I thought it would bother you, because you've always been religious. But I'm telling you now," said Una calmly. "I just can't believe that there's someone in heaven who controls everything we do."

Maisie was so shocked that it took her a few minutes to find an answer.

"I sometimes believe in God," said David. "As a scientist I think he's just a superstition, but when you see all this"—he pointed to the sky—"this . . . *glory*, it makes you think there might be something more."

"Exactly!" said Maisie. "There *is* something more! Una, how can you *not* believe, when the evidence is all around us? And I can't help being religious—my father is a rector! At least, he *was*," she added bitterly.

Una patted her knee. "I didn't mean to sound critical. You're perfectly free to believe whatever you want—I just happen not to. You've always liked church better than I have—I find it incredibly boring."

"I really enjoyed going to the service here," said

David. "Your grandfather is a wonderful preacher, Maisie. He's wasted in this tiny church."

"He's been offered jobs in bigger parishes," Maisie told him, "but he never wants to leave the island."

She turned to her cousin. "Una, two years ago when we were confirmed, you absolutely believed in God! I remember us talking about it. Maybe you should speak to Grand."

Una shook her head. "I couldn't do that—he'd just be hurt. And I don't need to, because I'm totally sure about this. It's okay, Maisie. I'll keep going to church as long as I live at home, because everyone expects me to. But when I'm an adult, I'll stop. Don't look so upset! We just have different beliefs, that's all."

"Well, *I* believe in God," said Maisie huffily. "I even . . ."

"What?" asked David.

"I even wish women could be ordained. I think it would be kind of interesting to be a rector."

Una giggled. "If you were ever a rector, Maise, then I *would* go to church just to see you dressed up in those crazy robes!"

"Maybe you can be, Maisie," said David. "Maybe one day the church will become more enlightened."

Maisie was so embarrassed she couldn't answer. She'd never told anyone this before. It was something she'd thought about for several years. As she'd sat and watched how woodenly Dad ran the Sunday services, she'd imagined how much better she herself could do it.

Could David be right? Could *she* become a rector? That seemed too impossible.

"I'm sorry if I've upset you, Maise," said Una. "I didn't mean to. I was just saying what I thought."

Maisie smiled at her. "You're entitled to your own beliefs just as I am to mine. It was just a surprise, that's all."

"*That's* all right, then," said David, appearing relieved. "You two are such good friends I don't want there to be any friction between you!"

They sat there a little longer in silent camaraderie. Maisie was sandwiched between the two of them, back to feeling safe and comfortable. They were pals.

❦

Granny and Grand returned the next day. "How was *Brigadoon*?" Maisie asked.

Granny sniffed. "So-so. You could certainly tell that the writer had never been to Scotland—it was nothing like it! It was a fantasy of Scotland, all misty and dreamy and sweet."

Grand winked at Maisie. "She loved every bit of it, and she hummed the songs all the way home."

"Well, the music *was* grand. We bought the record."

"Everyone in Vancouver is worried about the drought," Grand said. "They might try seeding the clouds to make it rain."

That evening Maisie had such bad cramps that she went to bed right after dinner. Granny had given her a shot of brandy. She lay cozily in the room off the kitchen—it was still too hot to sleep upstairs. Her grandparents were on the veranda, waiting for the sunset.

"Yoo-hoo!"

It was Polly at the back door. Granny came into the kitchen to greet her.

"I've come to borrow your big pot," said Polly. "I'm going to try making pickles for the fair. Where's Maisie? I wanted to tell her not to come tomorrow. I'm going to take Clary with me to Valencia Island."

"The poor lassie has such bad cramps I've sent her to bed," said Granny. "I dosed her with brandy, so I'm sure she's already asleep. I'll let her know. Would you like a cup of tea?"

They sat at the kitchen table, and their lazy chatter almost did send Maisie to sleep. But she woke up when she heard David's name.

"He's the bonniest lad I've ever laid eyes on!" raved Granny. "And a perfect young gentleman. This afternoon he saw me coming home from the store and insisted on carrying my groceries. Rachel and Ben have brought him up well, the way he calls Rand 'sir' and listens so respectfully to him. And he came to church! That's so polite of him when he isn't even Christian."

"He *is* a nice boy," agreed Polly. "Clary adores him, and he and Chester have become buddies, even though there's such an age gap between them. Chester says he's highly intelligent—he thinks he has a brilliant future."

Granny's voice became conspiratorial. "Of course it's much too early to even think of this, Polly, but wouldn't David make a wonderful match for one of the girls?"

"But they're still children!"

"I know . . . but he seems to like them both. We'll have to make sure they all keep in touch. Imagine my Maisie married to a distinguished astronomer! Or Una," she added hastily.

Polly laughed. "Aunt Jean, you are incorrigible! Let's just wait and see. The three of them certainly get along, anyway. And Una is always chattering about David. But it's just a friendship, and I hope it stays that way for now."

"Of course! Maisie and Una are as innocent as two lambs. And we certainly don't want to foster the situation that poor Maud found herself in. I'll never forget the morning she arrived on the island with that wee bairn in her arms!"

"Well, we got our precious Una out of it! And she's had such a secure childhood. Una will never be as foolish as Maud."

"That lass . . ." Granny sighed. "Look at her, with a man's job, consorting with murderers! I wish she could find a nice man and stop working."

Polly laughed. "Maud loves her work! Just like I do."

"Oh, well, what do I know? I'm just an old lady who's behind the times," she said complacently. "But tell me, Polly, does Maud have a man in her life? You would think she'd snatch up one of the lawyers she works with."

"She doesn't seem to, but she wouldn't tell me if she did. Maud has always been private."

"She must have been so hurt by Robert that she's afraid to risk another relationship. Imagine abandoning our Maud! What I would do to that man if I could get hold of him!"

"What are you two nattering about?" called Grand. "You're missing the best of the sunset!"

Maisie chuckled sleepily at Granny's projection for her future. She and David *married*—how absurd!

But it wasn't so absurd to imagine him and Una together. *Please, God, let Polly be right,* she prayed. *Please may Una and David just stay friends.*

༜

The next afternoon she and Una and David walked to the end of Ethel Point and back. They stopped halfway and ate their apples, gazing at a tiny island beyond the cliff. A group of seals always gathered there, balancing on the rocks like black commas. As the tide rose, they tumbled into the water at the last possible moment.

The grass was as crisp and tawny as shredded-wheat biscuits. David picked up a cigarette butt and flung it into the sea. "What imbecile left *this* here? One spark and the whole island could catch fire!"

"Grand says we've reached a record now," Maisie told him. "Over sixty days without rain!"

"*I* know!" said Una eagerly. "Let's make No Smoking signs and put them on the trails!"

"That's a terrific idea," said David.

They hurried home and borrowed Clary's crayons to do up some signs. Then they dashed around on their bikes, posting them on every trail they could think of. When they'd finished, they collapsed on the rectory veranda with some lemonade.

The steamer whistle blew, and Granny appeared. "Maisie, there's the mail. Would you go and fetch it for me? I'm too busy plucking these chickens."

"We'll all go," said David.

They meandered to the end of the wharf with the rest of the small crowd. David started talking to Captain Hay about his new tractor. Una spotted Doris and went over to ask her something.

Maisie watched the mailbag being lowered. The

crowd dwindled, as some of them left with passengers from the boat and others followed the mail to the store, where it would be sorted.

She noticed a man lingering by himself, looking uncertain. As she and Una and David turned to leave, the man approached them. He was about David's age, with a ruddy face and rough clothes.

"Hey, there—I need some help!" he said brusquely.

"What can we do for you?" asked David.

"I'm looking for a gal named Violet—Violet Crosby. Do you know where she lives? All I have is a box number."

Una gasped and put her hand to her mouth. Maisie just stared in horror.

"Do you know anyone of that name?" David asked them.

"No!" said Maisie tightly. "*Nobody* with that name lives here!"

"But she said Kingfisher Island!" said the man. "I have her letter in my pocket." He winked at David. "It's a real sweet one, I'll tell you."

"Get him to *leave*!" Una whispered to David.

"You must be wrong," David told the man. "My friends have been here all their lives, and they don't know anyone named Violet Crosby."

"Maybe they just haven't met her," said the man stubbornly. "She *must* be here."

"She isn't!" said Maisie.

"Ah, come on . . . I bet you know her and you're just protecting her. But don't you worry. I'm a good guy. I just want to lay my eyes on her, and then we'll see what happens . . ." He leered at David. "You know what I mean? Just ask your pretty girlfriends to tell me where she lives and I'll stop bothering you."

Now David was angry. "Listen here, chum. They've told you there's no one here with that name. I want you to get on that steamer before it leaves and go back where you came from. Otherwise I'll call the police!"

"Hey, you can't talk to me like that!"

David went closer and grabbed his shirt. "Sure I can. Are you going to get on the boat? Or am I going to send for the policeman?"

For a few seconds Maisie was terrified that the man was going to hit David. Then he looked sheepish.

"Ah, heck . . . I can't argue with you anymore. But what a bloody waste of cash, coming all the way over here for nothing." He turned away and trudged up the gangplank just in time.

The three of them watched in stunned silence as the steamer blew its whistle and thrummed away.

"What a chump! Why would he think that woman lived here? *Una* . . . what's wrong?"

Una was sobbing wildly. "Oh, David . . . it's all my fault! I did such a stupid, stupid thing!"

David led them to the coronation seat, and the whole story came out. *This is all Bev's fault,* thought Maisie, trying to stop her knees from shaking. How dare she get her and Una into such a scary situation?

At the end of the story David looked very serious. "That was a stupid thing to do. Don't you realize the danger you risked?"

Una wiped her eyes with her sleeve. "We didn't *think* it was dangerous. There was no way he could trace us, and we didn't expect him to actually come to the island!"

"But he did, didn't he? And of course it's dangerous, to write to a complete stranger. He could have gone to the postmistress and made up some story and traced you and come to your house! And it was mean to entice him to come all this way, no matter how unsavoury he was."

David was sounding way too much like an adult. Maisie squirmed. "It wasn't Una's fault! Her idiotic friend made her do it."

"Una didn't have to listen to her. And, Maisie, *you* could have stopped it. No one can make anyone do something if they don't want to. You both should have stood up to her."

Now Maisie was ashamed. She glanced at Una's pink cheeks and knew she was feeling the same. David was right: they could easily have squashed Bev's idea.

Finally David's stern look relaxed into a grim smile. "It was a stupid thing to do, but what a dumb guy to fall for it!"

"You were so brave!" said Una.

"You were," Maisie agreed. "I don't know what we would have done if you hadn't been there."

David chuckled. "We're lucky he didn't know there are no policemen on Kingfisher!"

"And we're lucky that no one in the family was there," said Una. "Promise you'll never tell?"

David paused for a few suspenseful seconds. "I *should* . . . but okay, I promise I won't."

❧

Everyone was busy preparing entries for the fall fair. Granny's kitchen was a flurry of canning and baking. Polly succeeded in making her pickles. Even Clary was participating—she was entering one of her drawings in the children's art category.

Maisie was desperately trying to finish the baby's sweater she had started in July. Granny was proud of her knitting. She had taught Maisie at age seven, and every year she came in first. Usually she enjoyed the rhythm of loading stitch upon stitch, but this year she was so tired of clicking the pink wool back and forth that she wanted to scream. It was tempting to give up the sweater altogether, but Granny would be hurt if she did.

"What are *you* entering, Una?" asked David.

"An apple pie. Bubby showed me how to make pastry. I hope it works, though. Every crust I've tried so far has been really tough."

David was examining the list of categories. "*I'm* going to enter!" he told them.

They gaped at him. "You are?"

"Yes! There's something in the art section called 'undressed driftwood.'"

Una giggled. "That sounds rude!"

"It's very, very serious," said David solemnly. "You find a piece of driftwood and say what you think it looks like. I've never been good at art, but this will be easy!"

They went to the beach and picked up driftwood. "This one is a mermaid!" said David.

"And here's Daisy Duck! And this one is a man with a top hat."

The more ridiculous they became the more they laughed. David and his mother were leaving this Saturday. Maisie realized how much she would miss him.

CHAPTER NINE

The Kiss (1)

"If this is what you're entering for the fair tomorrow, Aunt Jean, you'll win for sure," said Chester, pouring cream over his second piece of blueberry pie.

"I've entered all four categories," Granny told him. "Blueberry, raisin, lemon meringue, and apple."

"Your apple pie is sure to beat mine," said Una sadly. "The crust sort of fell apart—I had to put it on in patches."

"Never mind, pet, you're just learning," said her grandmother. "Anyway, yours is in the children's category. You won't be in the adult section until you're sixteen."

Maisie had spent all day finishing her sweater. She hadn't had time to wash it before she took it over to the hall. It was so grubby from being carried everywhere that she knew it wouldn't win anything, but she didn't care—at least it was done.

"Why is it called a 'fall fair,' when it's in August?" David asked.

"It's been that as long as I can remember," Grand told him.

"The old Gaelic calendar has August as the beginning of fall, not September," said Granny. "Winter begins in November, spring in February, and summer in May."

"I've never heard of that!" said David. "I'll tell my prof there's another way of naming the seasons besides astronomical and meteorological."

"Now, what on earth would *those* be?" asked Granny. David began a long explanation. Chester and Grand chimed in with their opinions, and David listened to them respectfully.

He was the star tonight. Everyone vied for his attention, as if he were royalty. Maisie watched the quiet pride on his mother's face and the adoration on Granny's. Then she glanced at Una. *Good* . . . she wasn't looking at David at all. Instead she was playing "Where is Thumbkin?" with Clary.

No one lingered long after dinner. Clary had fallen asleep on the sofa, and her parents took her home. Aunt Rachel said she had to finish packing; she left with Aunt Esther and Uncle Daniel.

"I'd better go and pack, as well," said David. "I'll see you all at the fair!"

Maud hadn't come home that weekend—she'd gone to visit some friends in Seattle. Granny and Grand went to sit on the veranda, and Maisie and Una volunteered to do the dishes. Then the two of them worked on the puzzle.

Maisie felt perfectly content. Her tedious knitting was done, her tummy was full of delicious food, and she was alone with her best friend. After David left, it would be just the two of them again. The only thing she dreaded was her parents' visit. That was still over a week away, however. And they would be so involved with the other adults that Maisie could easily escape them.

She gloated: her goal was achieved! Una and David had never been left alone, and Una's silly crush seemed to be over. She must have realized that David was much too old for her.

Una kept grabbing random puzzle pieces and trying them in impossible places. Her foot twitched, and her face was tense. Then she jumped up. "I'm going home now."

"But I thought we were going to sleep in the Hut!"

"Sorry, George, but I don't feel well. I think I'm getting my monthlies."

"Poor you." Maisie grinned. "Want a nip of Granny's

brandy? She'd be happy to give you some, and it works like a charm!"

Una smiled. "No, thanks. See you tomorrow!" She hurried away.

✌

For a while Maisie sat with her grandparents, but she, too, was restless. Walker Island had turned dark purple, and a few pink streaks were left in the sky. The enticing night seemed to be calling her to join it.

"I'm going for a walk," she announced.

"Wear a sweater," said Granny automatically. She had worked so hard that she was almost asleep in her chair.

"Don't forget your flashlight," said Grand.

Maisie kissed them goodnight, grabbed her sweater, thrust a small flashlight into her pocket, and set out along the road.

Which way should she go? If she went right, she would be more alone in the darkness, but something seemed to lead her left, towards the store and the hotel.

She glanced at Una's room as she passed her house. The light was already out—Una must have gone to bed. Through the window Maisie could see the silhouettes of Polly and Chester sitting with glasses of wine.

A bunch of island kids surrounded the bench outside the store. "Hey, Maisie, come and have a smoke!" called Doris.

Maisie knew she wouldn't really be welcome; anyway, she wanted to be alone. "No, thanks," she called back.

She walked out onto the wharf and stood there for a while, listening to the yip of otters on the rocks. The sea was a smooth navy blue, and the sky was thick with stars. There was the Big Dipper, and the Pleiades. Maisie tried to find Saturn, as David had instructed them, but she couldn't pick it out. She gave up and just gazed at the Milky Way. When she was little, she had really believed it was a glass of milk that God had spilled across the sky.

Then a star streaked across—and another! Of course—tonight was the peak of the Perseid meteor shower. David had planned for them all to stay up past midnight and watch it. He must have forgotten.

I'll stay up, Maisie decided. Midnight must be only an hour or so away. And she couldn't bear to go in. If only she could wrap up this magical summer night and keep it to comfort her in the winter.

She reached the hotel, glimpsing a few more darting stars as she walked. Some of the guests were chattering on the veranda:

"And she never paid me back!"

". . . all veiny and swollen."

"Was that the really tall guy?"

How silly people sounded! Maisie walked past them and up the hill that led away from the hotel and along the shore. Now it was dark enough to use her flashlight. She and Una used to sneak out of bed on nights like this and be detectives, lighting up the road and looking for clues. How free it had felt to wander around in the dark without the grown-ups knowing! But they probably did know, she realized now. The island was so safe they let them be.

It was silent now, and the brilliant stars seemed to hum above her. *Hoo*-hoo-hoo-*hoooo*, called a distant owl.

Maisie spread her arms, as if she were embracing the whole peaceful island. *If only I could live here all the time,* she thought.

Then she had a marvellous idea. Maybe, when she was an adult, she *could*! Maybe she could take care of Granny and Grand when they were old. After they died—a *terrible* thought, but it was going to happen one day—she could live in their house.

But if she never married, she wouldn't have a husband to support her. What would she do for a living?

Make things . . . the idea seized her so strongly that Maisie chuckled out loud. People always needed shelves or tables or birdhouses. She could sell them at the store! And she could fix sagging doors and broken fences, and construct gates. She didn't know how to do all those things, but she could learn.

That's what I'm going to do! Maisie told David in her head. *I'm going to be a carpenter!* Despite what he had said, it didn't seem possible that women could ever be rectors; but she didn't see why they couldn't be carpenters. For the first time since Dad had become ill, the future didn't look bleak.

She was approaching a steep narrow path that led down to a cove. Maisie decided to sit there for a while, to contemplate these exciting plans that seemed to have zoomed into her mind like the shooting stars.

Her light led her down to the beach. At the far end she spotted two distant figures sitting on a log. Maisie halted and tried to make out who they were, but all she could see were their dark backs. It was tempting to light them up with her flashlight, but that would startle them.

She could tell from their outlines that the couple was a boy and a girl—probably guests from the hotel. Maisie watched, both fascinated and repulsed, as they stopped whispering and began a lingering kiss.

Then they drew apart, and a voice rang out clearly: "Oh, *David!*"

CHAPTER TEN

The Letter

Maisie didn't know how she got home. After stumbling into bed with her clothes on, she plunged into sleep. Maybe what she had witnessed would turn out to have been a dream.

But when she awoke, the relentless fact was waiting for her: *Una and David had kissed.*

Somehow she got through the motions of eating breakfast and accompanying her grandparents to the fair. Standing beside Granny at the children's handicraft display, she felt like a sleepwalker. Her knitting hadn't won a ribbon, of course. It slumped on the table, grimy and ashamed, among the pristine winning garments.

"Oh, chickie, you should have given me your sweater to wash!" scolded Granny.

"There wasn't time," mumbled Maisie.

They wandered around the crowded room, examining the rest of the entries. Long tables were spread with produce, homemade wine, floral arrangements, baked goods, honey, jams and jellies, and arts and crafts. People jostled and exclaimed as they leaned in to see who had won each category.

"Seven ribbons—that's a record for me!" gloated Granny. "And this year I beat Mildred in canning *and* needlepoint." She frowned when they reached the pie section. The First Prize ribbon had been awarded to a Mrs. Hastie.

"Humph," Granny sniffed. "I don't think summer people should be allowed to enter, do you, chickie?"

Maisie was too distracted to remind Granny that *she*, Maisie, was a summer person. She was scanning the crowd for Una. To her relief, she couldn't see her anywhere. And David was absent, as well, even though there was a blue ribbon on his piece of driftwood labelled *Sad Donkey*—the only entry in the "undressed" category.

I bet they're together, she thought bitterly. *Everyone else is at the fair, and they're alone in Una's room,* kissing . . .

Rage filled Maisie like foul black bile. She escaped from the suffocating crowd and went out to sit under the trees in the grounds, away from the people buying lunch at the tables selling sandwiches and drinks.

Why am I so angry? she wondered, fanning her hot face. After all, it was perfectly normal for teenagers to kiss each other!

It was partly their deception. They must have been secretly meeting the whole time David was visiting. Perhaps at the hotel in the mornings, and in the evenings when she and Una didn't sleep in the Hut. Maisie tried to remember how many of those there were. She imagined how Una would tell the adults she was going for a walk to look at the stars, how she would meet David at the cove every time, how eagerly they would embrace . . .

And last night . . . of *course* Una was agitated; of *course* she said she was sick! Maisie almost gagged.

She should have told me! thought Maisie. But would she be any happier if Una had? It wasn't just the deception; it was the fact that Una wanted to be with someone other than her. It was like when Bev was here, but far, far worse.

Maisie wiped her eyes with her sleeve. *What's the matter with me? Una is my best friend! Surely I should be happy she has a boyfriend.*

"Maisie, what are you doing out here all by yourself?" Polly and Clary were standing in front of her.

"I won First Prize, Maisie!" crowed Clary. She was holding a painting of orange-and-purple smears. A blue ribbon was attached to it.

Maisie tried to smile.

"She wasn't supposed to take away her painting, but she refused to leave it," said Polly.

"Where's Una?" Maisie forced herself to ask. "I didn't see her in there."

"She had cramps, so she stayed in bed."

Cramps sure were handy sometimes. When Una *really* got her monthlies, everyone was going to wonder why it happened so often.

Maisie wanted to know why David wasn't here, either, but she couldn't form the words.

❧

David and his mother were supposed to leave on the late-afternoon steamer. Maisie spent all afternoon on the swinging chair on the veranda, escaping into a childhood book. *Not* Nancy Drew. She was never going to read those books again! How could she have forgotten that Nancy had a boyfriend named Ned?

Instead Maisie chose her favourite, *Stuart Little*, taking a bit of comfort in the chivalrous mouse and his adventures. Granny and Grand were visiting the Cunninghams, and the house was quiet and peaceful. The living room clock chimed out the creeping time.

Just three more hours . . . just two more . . . just an hour and a half and he'll be gone . . . David and his mother planned to stay in Vancouver tonight and take the train to Boston tomorrow morning. At least that was far away from Una. But they could write to each other and plan to meet again. Or Una could beg to go and see him while she and Maud were in Toronto . . .

Stop thinking about it! Maisie finished her book with a gulp. How sad the ending was! The little mouse was headed north, still seeking his lost love.

"Maisie?"

David!

He stood on the veranda steps hesitantly. "May I sit down?" he asked.

What could she say? She nodded.

David looked awful. Purple smudges curved under his eyes, and his usually clean hair hung in greasy strings.

"Una isn't here," muttered Maisie.

"I know. I need to talk to you alone."

Despite herself, Maisie couldn't help giving in to the desperate look in his intense eyes. "What about?" she asked.

"Well, it's kind of awkward. I need you to do me a favour. Will you?"

Didn't that depend on what it was? But again, Maisie had to nod.

David pulled an envelope out of his pocket. "This is a letter for Una, but I don't want her to read it until after I've left. Would you give it to her tonight?"

Maisie took the envelope. "All right," she said slowly. "But why are you writing her a letter when you're still here?"

David looked so lost. "I just am. *Please,* Maisie, can you get it to her? I'd be so grateful if you could."

"Sure, it's no problem."

"Thanks, Maise, you're a chum!" He stood up. "We're leaving soon. Are you coming to the wharf to see us off?"

"Probably not. I have to—to pick some beans for dinner." That sounded so lame, but she couldn't think of another excuse.

"Then I'll say goodbye now. I've really enjoyed getting to know you, Maisie—you're a good kid."

He patted her awkwardly on the shoulder. Then he walked rapidly down the steps and along the road.

Maisie sat there until he was out of sight. Then she ran into the house to open the letter.

§

Of *course* she shouldn't . . . but she was beyond caring about right and wrong. She had to do it carefully, however, so Una wouldn't notice. *Steam!* That's what people in books used to open letters.

First she had to make a small fire in the stove. Once the kettle was boiling she held the envelope over the steaming spout. *Ouch!* Her fingers burned, and she had to keep pulling them away. The envelope wrinkled alarmingly, but finally the glue loosened enough so she could carefully peel open the flap.

She took the letter to the Hut—in case Granny and Grand returned. Then she removed it from the envelope. Her hands trembled—what words would the two sheets contain?

Dear, sweet Una,

I'm so sorry I rushed away from you like that, but I couldn't stay. I shouldn't have kissed you. I'm five years older than you are! That's why I left. Our kisses were going on and on and I never wanted to stop, but I knew that was wrong.

When we met at Dad's funeral, I was amazed at how much you had grown up. I loved our conversation—you were so kind to me in my grief. I've enjoyed spending time with you on the island and getting to know you better. But until last night, I just thought of you as a friend.

Now all that has changed. You looked so incredibly beautiful, sitting there under the stars, that when you asked me to kiss you, I couldn't resist.

When I got back to my room, I sat up all night and tried to sort out my feelings. Dad always told me to be absolutely honest with people, so that's what I'm trying to be. It's very simple, really. I'm falling in love with you! You are so special, Una— not only beautiful, but kind and talented and fun to be with.

But you're just an innocent kid! I have no right to ask any commitments of you, but I also don't want to lose the possibility that perhaps one day we could have a relationship. So I have a request. Una, my sweet girl, could we wait until you've finished high school and then see how we feel about each other? It wouldn't be proper for us to meet before then, but perhaps we could write. If, in three years, you feel the same way about me as I do about you, perhaps we could try getting together again.

Let me know what you think. I've written my Boston address below—we should be there by next weekend. If I don't hear from you, then I'll know you don't feel the same about me as I do about you. I will respect that, and I won't write again.

I gave this letter to Maisie for you to open tonight. She's a good friend to you, and I don't mind if you show it to her. I know you won't tell anyone else in the family. How they would disapprove! I don't blame them. You're far too young for me to ask anything of you. I shouldn't even *be writing this letter, but I can't bear to lose the possibility, however slight, that we might one day be together.*

How I hope you will write back!

Much love,
David

Maisie gulped in air—she had been holding her breath the whole time she'd been reading the letter. She read it twice more, each word seared in her brain. Only one thought possessed her: *Una must not read this!*

Crumpling the letter and envelope, she ran to the house. She paused at the back door as she heard the whistle of the steamer. Granny and Grand weren't back—they would have gone down to the wharf to say goodbye.

The stove was still hot from boiling the kettle. Maisie lifted one of the stovetop covers and dropped the letter into the embers. It blazed up quickly. She watched until the little fire had turned to cinders, until she was certain that not one inky word remained. After spreading out the ashes, she replaced the cover.

Then she went out to pick the beans.

CHAPTER ELEVEN

A Lost Sheep

The next morning Granny asked, "Rand, have you written to the dean yet?"

"I have, but don't get your hopes up, my dear. All the seats may be taken."

"But you and Ernie Lloyd are old friends! Surely he can arrange something for us. Perhaps you should telephone him."

"I'm certain a letter will be fine. It's not until October, after all."

Princess Elizabeth and Prince Philip were coming to Canada. They would spend seven days on the coast, and while they were in Vancouver would attend a church service at the cathedral. Granny was determined that Canon Lloyd, the dean, would reserve them a seat.

"Who cares if you get seats or not?" snapped Maisie. "Why should it be such a big deal? They're just people!"

"Maisie, how can you say that—she is a *princess*!"

"Sorry, Granny," she muttered. "I know how much they mean to you. They just don't to me, that's all."

Granny looked hurt. "They did once. You used to *love* looking at my scrapbooks!"

"Maisie is entitled to her own opinion," said Grand. "But perhaps you could express it a little more gently," he added.

She apologized again and fled the breakfast table. If this tiny issue could disappoint them, what would they think if they knew what she had done?

❧

Maisie waited anxiously for Una to tell her everything about the kiss. She managed to avoid her all morning, but after lunch Una appeared at the door.

"Are you feeling better, chickie?" asked Granny. "How glad I am that I don't have to endure my monthly visitor anymore!"

Una blushed. "I'm fine, Aunt Jean. Maisie, come for a walk."

Maisie had never been a good actor. Some of her friends yearned for parts in the school play; she always volunteered to work behind the scenes.

But now she had to force herself into the disguise of the kind and sympathetic cousin. She listened and nodded and made appropriate soothing comments as they sat in the Hut and Una poured it all out.

She went into every detail. How she'd grown fonder of David every moment, how she just couldn't tell if he felt the same.

"On Friday I felt so desperate—David was leaving the next day and I might never see him again! So before dinner I asked him to go for a walk later, so he could show me the meteor shower."

"But we were *all* going to do that!"

"Sorry, Maise. But it was the only way I could think of to see David alone—we never had been."

Maisie flinched; so Una hadn't deceived her after all! "Did you have a good time?" was all she could think of replying.

"Oh, George—it was the best night of my life! At first we were kind of awkward, but then I felt more and more comfortable with him. We talked and talked, the way we did at the funeral. I felt as if I had known David forever. We went down to that little cove past the hotel. The waves were all sparkly. We dipped our hands in the water and made designs. David was really interested in the luminescence, of course. He said it was light given off by plankton in the water. What a lot he knows!"

Just get on with it! thought Maisie, but of course Una wanted to linger over every moment.

"David was really quiet for a while. He looked *so* handsome and I just . . . *longed* for him so much that I—well, I asked him if he would kiss me! He seemed kind of surprised. But then—oh, Maisie, he *did*!"

Maisie tried not to look away from her friend's radiant face.

"It was *amazing*—better than all the love songs. We just kept kissing and kissing. It made me tingle all over my body, and I wanted it to go on forever. But then David jumped up and ran away! I don't know what happened! Did I do something wrong?"

Then the tears came. Maisie patted Una's shoulder as she sobbed. "The next morning I was afraid to see David in front of everyone—I thought they would all be able to tell how I felt. So I pretended I was sick. What was he like at the fair, Maisie? Did he seem unhappy?"

"He wasn't at the fair," she muttered.

"He wasn't? Then he must have stayed at the hotel! Oh, if only I'd gone over there then he could have explained!"

"Did you go to the wharf?"

"No! I intended to, but I thought he'd come over and say goodbye. When he didn't, I thought he didn't want to see me. But *why not?*" Una mopped

144

her face with her handkerchief. "Did *you* go to the wharf?"

Maisie shook her head.

"I know he and his mother took the train to Boston today," said Una. She grabbed Maisie's hand. "Do you think he *knows*?"

"What do you mean?"

"That I'm illegitimate! His parents may have told him. Do you think that while he was kissing me, he was afraid I'd want to go all the way like Mum did, and that's why he ran away?"

Maisie frowned. "What do you mean, 'go all the way'?" She'd never heard that expression before. How had Una? At school, probably—city kids were more knowing than small-town kids like her.

"You know—have sex. Maybe David thinks I'll be like Mum and want to have intercourse before I'm married. Maybe he thinks I'm cheap. But I'm not!"

"Una, how can you talk that way! You're not cheap, and neither is Maud! She just made a mistake. *You* told me that!"

Una sighed. "You're right. That was a dumb thing to say. But why did he run away then, when it was so magical? And why didn't he say goodbye?"

She began to cry again, and this time Maisie couldn't touch her shaking body. Instead she hugged her own shoulders and despised herself. Her stomach churned, and she thought she might throw up.

What had she done? At that moment she would have given anything to have the letter back.

So why didn't she simply confess?

Because then Una would hate her. Maisie couldn't risk her rejection, even though that meant Una was unaware that she was crying for nothing—that David was falling in love with her. That's how despicable Maisie was being. She was putting herself before her best friend's happiness.

Una sat up, wiped her eyes, and tried to smile. "David *must* have a good reason for what happened. He'll probably write and explain. I *know* he will! And if he doesn't, I'll write to *him*."

Oh, no! Maisie hadn't thought of this. But she hadn't thought of anything when she burned the letter—she had just acted on her basest instincts, as if possessed by a demon.

If Una wrote to David, he'd ask why Maisie hadn't given her his letter. Then she would *have* to confess. Una would hate her even more for not telling her earlier.

Whatever happened now, Maisie was going to lose her.

Polly and Chester and Clary left for a two-week drive down the Oregon coast to visit Chester's parents, who had moved off the island last summer. That meant that Maisie had a holiday, too.

She tried to avoid Una by working on Granny's bookcase. She had drawn a plan and sawed pieces for the sides, back, and shelves from leftover lumber. But now she was having a terrible time trying to cut dado joints for the shelves. She tried to remember how Dad did it. If only he were here to help!

"How it's going, George?" Una pushed through the door.

Oh, no! Maisie didn't answer. Maybe if she ignored her, Una would go away.

But she leaned over the worktable. "What's that?" she asked.

"A router plane," muttered Maisie.

"What's it for?"

"It's for cutting a dado joint, but I don't think I've measured this one right."

"What's a dado joint?"

"A groove for the shelf to fit into." Maisie looked up, wiping sweat from her eyes. "Una, it's *really* hard to concentrate when you're hanging over me!"

"Then I'll stop bothering you!"

Una fled, and Maisie put down her tools. Now she wiped away tears. How could she hurt Una even more?

To make up, she forced herself to ask Una to pick blackberries with her. Their hands turned purple as they dropped juicy berries into pails hung by string around their necks. Una kept agonizing to Maisie about David. Each word pricked as sharply as the vicious thorns.

Una was first on the wharf on Boat Day, waiting for David's letter. Maisie tried to reassure her that it was too soon to expect it.

"I should just write to *him*," Una said again.

"I wouldn't," said Maisie. "You—you shouldn't look too eager. Isn't that what the advice columns say? Wait for him to write first."

How could she mouth such drivel? But she was desperate.

Every morning she woke up with the same resolve: *Today I'll tell her.* In a few words she could clear the misery from Una's beautiful grey eyes. But Maisie was too much of a coward to utter the words.

She was so miserable herself that she couldn't get up in the mornings and appeared late at the breakfast table, bleary eyed and numb.

"What's wrong with you, chickie?" asked Granny.

She made Maisie have a spoonful of her horrible homemade tonic made of onions, horseradish root, and cider vinegar.

"Perhaps you're worried about your parents arriving," said Grand. "Are you, dear?"

Maisie kept forgetting that Mum and Dad were coming on Monday. She tried to smile at Grand. "Of course not—I'm looking forward to seeing them."

He was so kind. Could she tell him the truth?

Every Sunday for most of her life Maisie had chanted "'We have erred, and strayed from thy ways like lost sheep. We have followed too much the devices and desires of our own hearts . . . we have done those things which we ought not to have done.'"

That was confessing to God. Maisie had never paid much attention to those words before, but on the Sunday after she had burned the letter she said them fervently. And every night she prayed, "*Help* me, God. Help me have the courage to tell Una."

But God didn't seem to be helping at all. Could Grand? Could she confess to *him*? Tell him what she had done and ask him what to do?

Grand thought she was perfect, however. Maisie couldn't bear to disappoint him.

"If you don't stop being so sleepy you'll have to go to see Dr. Cunningham," Granny told her.

The next morning Maisie stumbled out of bed at her usual time.

Then Maud decided to take Una to Vancouver. She asked Maisie to come along. "Una and I will stay until Friday, but you could come back in a few days to spend time with your parents. You're both looking so peaky you need a change. We can go to the PNE and Theatre Under the Stars. While I'm at work, you two can explore downtown, and you can see as many movies as you like."

How Maisie would have adored this any other summer! "Thanks for asking," she mumbled, "but I should be here when Mum and Dad arrive."

"I'm so sorry you can't come, but at least you can watch out for David's letter," Una told her. "Phone me the minute it arrives and you can read it to me."

Maisie hugged her and waved to them from the wharf. What a relief it was not to have to keep looking at Una's stricken face!

ஃ

That night she moved back to her attic room and helped Granny change the sheets for her parents. Maisie could hardly take it in that they were arriving the next day.

"I'm glad so many members of the family will be away this week," said Granny. "That will be quieter for Gregor. But everyone will be back for their anniversary dinner on Friday. Do you think your father will mind a big crowd?"

Maisie had no idea what Dad would mind. "Maybe it will cheer him up," she said dully.

That's what Granny wanted to hear.

"I agree! Once my dear boy is in the midst of us all he's going to feel much better."

She took Maisie into the backyard and cut her hair. "You'll want to look tidy for your parents," she said.

When she was done, she fluffed up Maisie's curls and said fondly, "There! You're my bonny wee lassie again!"

If only she was! If only she was still the innocent, good child whom Granny doted upon! Instead of this *lump*, who had betrayed her best friend.

"Why, chickie—you're crying!" said Granny.

Maisie tried to smile. "No, I'm not. It's just the sun in my eyes."

CHAPTER TWELVE

At the Lighthouse

Maisie's parents had arranged to come to the island on a friend's private boat—"because your dad wouldn't be able to bear the crowded steamer," Mum had said on the phone.

Now Mum stood on the wharf and hugged Maisie, tears in her eyes. "Oh, pickle, how I've missed you!"

Dad kissed her forehead mechanically. He looked sad and bewildered and distant, as if he didn't know where he was.

Granny clung to his arm fiercely. "Now, Gregor, I want you to just rest while you're here. You don't have to do a thing!"

"Lucky you," joked Grand. "You'll be the first male in history your mother has allowed to sit still!"

His son didn't respond; he didn't even look at him.

He's only trying to cheer you up! thought Maisie. She felt so numb herself, however, that she couldn't even feel angry.

As the day wore on, Maisie observed how shocked her grandparents were at their son's condition. He established himself on a chair on the veranda and barely moved from it. Granny kept offering him books or tea or her chattering company; Grand suggested a walk and a boat ride. Dad just grunted refusals.

I could have told you how hopeless he is, thought Maisie. But Granny and Grand were such optimists they wouldn't have believed her. It broke her heart to watch their offers being repulsed.

Mum clung to Maisie thirstily, asking her countless questions about her summer. What could she say? That she had destroyed Una's happiness? That she didn't understand why she had done what she had, that she felt like a monster? What would Mum think about her then? She answered as shortly as possible and felt as detached as Dad.

At dinner Granny prattled desperately to Mum about the fair, while the men sat silently, both hardly eating. Maisie gazed at her miserable family. Couldn't anyone *do* anything?

She went to bed early just to escape from them all. *Why aren't you listening to me, God?* she prayed. *Dad is a mess, and everyone else is unhappy. I hate myself for what I did. So* help *me, God! If you don't, I'm going to stop believing in you.*

Her bitter words shocked her. Could she truly do that? Was she going to lose God along with Una? Now she felt even more like a lost sheep.

ℱ⌀

The next morning Maisie sprawled in the living room, wishing Clary were back so she'd have something to do. Granny and Mum were cleaning the church silver. Maisie should go over and help, but her misery froze her. Dad and Grand had claimed the veranda, so she couldn't go out there to read. She didn't want to be with anyone, but she didn't want to be alone—then her guilt would consume her.

She fetched her hat and decided to go to the store for candy. On the way out she glanced back. Grand was deep in his paper and Dad was gazing at the sea with his usual blank expression.

All at once Maisie was so angry at him that she actually shook. She ran back up the stairs. "Dad!" she shouted.

Grand looked up with surprise, and Dad was so startled that he flinched.

"Oh! Good morning, Maisie."

Maisie tried to steady her voice. "Come for a walk," she told him firmly. The doctor had said that

155

Dad was supposed to walk every day, but he hadn't once since he'd quit the church. Well, it was about time he did!

"No, thank you."

"*Yes!* I haven't seen you all summer! We can go to the lighthouse."

Dad seemed to shake himself awake. "Well, that would be nice, I suppose."

Maisie held the door open. Grand beamed with approval while Dad stumbled down the stairs and blinked in the glaring sun.

"It's so hot," he said with surprise, as they trudged along the road.

"Of *course* it's hot!" snapped Maisie. "Wasn't it in Duncan?" When Dad didn't answer, she forced her voice to be less angry. "The island is having a terrible drought. Granny is almost out of water for the garden, and she's worried that she'll lose all her vegetables."

When Dad still didn't answer, Maisie gave up talking to him. It was just a waste of words. They reached the lighthouse and sat silently on a bench in the shade. A few summer people carrying a picnic basket smiled as they passed by. They thought Dad and Maisie were a normal father and daughter sharing time together. No one knew that one of them was crazy and the other a thief.

❧

Dad seemed exhausted when they got home. He went into his room and shut the door. Mum and Granny were in the kitchen.

"Oh, pickle!" Mum hugged her. "Do you know how many times I've tried to get your father to take a walk? You are a miracle!"

Maisie felt a tiny glow of satisfaction. She was a liar, a destroyer of private property, and a terrible friend, but at least she could do *something* right.

For the rest of the week she had a mission: to walk her father every day, as if he were a dog. He only wanted to go to the lighthouse, even though Maisie suggested other routes. It took over an hour, since they sat for so long.

Maisie had another goal: to force her father to talk. She began to ask him questions, mostly about his boyhood on the island. She was so direct that he had no choice but to answer. At first it was in clipped words, but the more Maisie asked, the longer his sentences became.

"Tell me what you did in the summers," she said.

"Oh, nothing much."

"But what? Did you have a boat?"

"Yup."

"What kind of boat?"

"We had two—the gasboat and the rowboat."

"Where did you go in them?"

Dad shrugged.

"No, *tell* me," insisted Maisie—as if Dad were Clary. "Tell me one place where you went in the rowboat."

Dad's face became less vacant. "Well, one time I tried to row all the way around St. Mark Point. But the sea became too rough to carry on, and when I turned back, the tide was against me, and I couldn't make any progress. So I had to row ashore and tie the boat to a tree."

Maisie chuckled. "Una and I did the same thing last summer. Granny was mad at us because she wanted the boat for a picnic."

Dad actually smiled. "She was mad at me, as well."

On the next walk Dad told Maisie about sneaking into the church with his friends and drinking the Communion wine. "We replaced it with grape juice," he said. "Either my father didn't notice, or he decided not to say anything."

"He probably knew," said Maisie. "Grand notices everything."

When Dad opened up like this, their conversation seemed almost normal.

It wasn't like *Before*, of course. Maisie remembered sitting on this same bench with Dad when she was six. All the women in the family had gone over to Valencia Island to a baby shower, and Dad had been in charge of her. First they went swimming; Dad began to teach

Maisie the crawl. Then they dug for clams, shrieking each time they squirted. Afterwards Dad made her a wonderful lunch that consisted solely of Granny's left-over raisin scones, toasted and spread with blackberry jam. After lunch he'd read her some of *Stuart Little* and they'd both fallen asleep on the sofa. Then they walked to the lighthouse and were lucky enough to see a pod of leaping orcas. They played hide-and-seek all over the lighthouse grounds. Then they rested on this bench, Maisie collapsing in giggles as Dad told her "The Three Little Pigs," huffing and puffing with vigour and encouraging her to do the same. Finally they had gone home. Maisie sat the whole way on Dad's shoulders—she was light enough then—clutching his thatch of curls and feeling as tall as a giant.

She shooed the memory from her head. Dad was nowhere near the jolly, lively father from *Before*— would he ever be? But he *was* improving. He still clammed up on some of their walks, but he began to talk a bit at the dinner table, and once again everyone praised Maisie.

෨ৎ

Maisie's father's fragile progress was halted when everyone arrived back on Friday. Granny had planned the huge celebration meal all week.

"Remember those disgusting wartime cakes?" she asked Mum, as they made icing for the anniversary cake.

Mum grimaced. "How could I forget? Eggless, milkless, butterless, and no white sugar!"

Maisie was licking the beater. "What was in them then?"

"Hot water, brown sugar, lard, raisins, flour, baking soda, cinnamon, and cloves," recited Granny. "It *looked* like a cake, but it certainly wasn't!"

"Don't you remember rationing, pickle?" asked Mum. "Sugar, tea and coffee, butter and meat . . . and chocolate bars!"

"I remember not being able to buy *them*," said Maisie. It was soothing to help in the kitchen. But tonight Una would be back, and Maisie's guilt would suffocate her once again.

§

Una had had her perm cut off in Vancouver. Now she looked like her old self, her cap of smooth hair framing her face.

"Still no letter!" she whispered to Maisie, after Grand had said grace.

All Maisie could do was try to smile, while she stuffed herself with as much of the fabulous food as possible.

At the end of the feast Granny marched in proudly with the cake. She had iced "Happy Anniversary, Sadie and Gregor" on it. There was even champagne. Maisie and Una were allowed to have one glass. Its fizzy sweetness tickled Maisie's nose.

"I had *my* first champagne at your wedding, Sadie," said Polly. "What a wonderful day that was!"

They all drank a toast. Everyone pretended not to notice Mum's frozen smile and the fact that Dad had not spoken a word during the whole meal. Clary seemed to sense his reserve and didn't go near him. Just as Granny had feared, the impact of the whole family at once was too overwhelming. *Were all those walks for nothing?* thought Maisie.

"*I* want some of that drink!" said Clary.

Her father took her on his knee and gave her a tiny sip. They all laughed as she wrinkled her nose. Chester began to croon "*A*, you're adorable," and everyone sang along—everyone but Dad.

"The men are doing the dishes!" announced Chester. "Come on, Gregor. Let's lead the way." He and Dad and Grand and Uncle Daniel left the room.

"I hope they don't break anything," said Granny. "And they won't know where anything goes."

"It's good for them," said Polly. "Chester always helps me do the dishes."

"So does Daniel," said Aunt Esther. "Times have

changed, Jean. We've been spoiling our men for too long."

Maud's arm embraced Mum's shoulders. "I've taken the whole week off so I can spend time with you. Let's go for a long walk tomorrow. We have so much to talk about!"

Of course they were going to discuss Dad. Maisie wondered if Maud had suggested a psychiatrist yet.

Una beckoned her to the veranda. "Oh, George, I don't know what to do!" she moaned. "Should *I* write?"

Maisie's heart thudded. "Whatever you want," she muttered.

Una nibbled her finger. "I think I won't. If David hasn't written, then he obviously doesn't like me. Maybe *that's* why he ran away and never said goodbye. Maybe after he kissed me he decided I wasn't for him after all. Well, I'm not going to beg."

She looked so proud, even though her lip was trembling: like a noble young prince with a shiny helmet of hair.

Maisie knew exactly what she should say: "Una, let's go out to the Hut. I have something to tell you."

But once again, she couldn't do it.

❧

Walking with Dad the next afternoon gave Maisie an excuse to avoid Una. She was surprised when he began talking without prompting.

"Maud looks so well," he said, "and she's made such a success of her life. Unlike me," he added mournfully.

This was the first time Dad had talked about the present. What could Maisie say that wouldn't upset him?

"You *were* a success . . ." she said slowly. "And you will be again, I'm sure."

He shook his head. "There's nothing left for me now." His tone was so hopeless and resigned. What darkness did he reside in?

They were both in darkness. Despite Maisie "doing him good," as Granny said, Dad seemed more despairing than ever. And Maisie's agony was even worse now that Una was back.

She looked at Dad's glum face. Why not tell *him* her predicament? He wasn't the only person with problems! Why should *he* get all the attention? Maybe he could be a real dad again. Maybe he could even tell her what to do.

"Dad?" she ventured.

"Uh-huh?"

"There's something I need to tell you. It's about something I did that was really wrong."

Dad looked frightened. "I'm not a good person to talk to, I'm afraid."

"But you're my father!"

He looked even more scared. "Maisie—I—I can't cope. Talk to your grandfather. I'm sure he can help."

"I don't *want* to talk to Grand—I want to talk to
you!"

"No, Maisie."

He edged away from her on the bench—as if she
were dangerous!

Maisie sprang up. "All I want is for you to be my
dad!" she cried. "But you haven't been that since you
came back from the war. I'm your *daughter*! I *need* you!
And you just sit around like a stupid lump and expect
us all to take care of you. All week I've tried and tried
to help you. Well, I'm not going to any more!"

She ran away from him—all the way down the
road, behind the rectory and through the trees to the
Hut. Her chest heaved, and it felt as though her heart
was going to burst into pieces. She collapsed on the
mattress, and sobbed until she fell asleep.

CHAPTER THIRTEEN

Two Confessions

After Maisie woke up, she stumbled into the rectory, to find everyone in an uproar.

"Where have you *been*, chickie? We've been calling and calling you!" said Granny.

"Where is your father?" asked Mum. Her face was pale.

"*I* don't know. I left Dad at the lighthouse. He—he wanted to stay longer so I came back without him."

"It's almost seven o'clock, and he hasn't come home!"

Why did Mum look so frantic? "You were so late that I rode your bike to the lighthouse to find you. No one was there! Your grandfather and Chester have gone in the car to look for you both. I was hoping you'd be together. Gregor must be alone out there somewhere!"

Maisie shrugged. Why was Mum making such a fuss? "Well, Dad couldn't have gone far. It's a small island. And he won't get lost—he grew up here!"

"Pickle . . ." Mum took her by the hand and led her to the sofa. "You know that we never leave your father alone—but I've never told you why. He can't be left in case . . . in case he harms himself."

Maisie was so bleary from sleep she could hardly take in her mother's words. "What do you mean, harms himself?"

Mum started to cry. Granny sat down on the other side of Maisie and took her hand.

"Chickie, it means that your dad is so unhappy that he might try to take his own life. That's why we're so worried."

Now Maisie was jolted awake. "*Take his own life* . . . you mean, *suicide?*"

Granny shuddered. "Yes, but I'm sure he won't. I'm sure Gregor just went for a long walk. Now, Maisie, come and eat—we saved some chicken salad for you."

Maisie wolfed down salad and bread. Then they sat on the veranda and waited, sipping tea. For Mum's sake, Maisie tried to be calm, but inside she seethed with worry. What had she done? How could she have told Dad those horrible things? If he did what they feared—if he *killed* himself—it would be all her fault!

But just as Walker Island darkened against the rosy sky, Dad walked up the stairs with the others.

"Oh, *Gregor* . . ." Mum ran into his arms. "Where have you *been*?"

He hugged her briefly, then released her and looked at them all. "I decided to see how far I could walk around the island," he said quietly. "Sorry I caused you such worry. I'm going to bed now."

"But don't you want anything to eat?" asked Granny.

"No, thanks, Ma. See you in the morning."

Dad went into the bedroom and closed the door.

"Where did you find him?" asked Mum in a low voice, as they settled on the veranda again.

"Coming up from Fowler Bay," said Chester. "Gregor seemed all right, Sadie. A bit dazed, but calm. He said he didn't realize how late it was, and he apologized for making us go out to look for him."

"He sounded better than he has since he arrived," said Grand. "More like his old self!"

"Well, at least he's home safely and we can all stop worrying," said Granny. "I think we all need a wee drop of brandy."

Maisie had some, too. It burned all the way down and made her so sleepy that she curled up with her head in Mum's lap. Mum stroked her hair.

"I'll bunk in with you tonight, pickle," she whispered. "We'll let Dad sleep in peace."

All night Mum pressed against Maisie's back in the narrow bed, holding her close.

※

Grand was right: the next morning Dad did seem improved. He was still very quiet, but he paid more attention. He took his dishes to the sink, and he even asked Granny if she wanted him to cut some kindling.

"Yes, please, my precious laddie!" Her face beamed as Dad went out to the woodpile.

Maisie was as relieved as anyone else that Dad was safe, and of course she was glad that he seemed a bit better. Most of all, she was thankful that her outburst hadn't made him do the worst. Already those words "take his own life" seemed impossible.

They should have told me, she thought resentfully. *If I'd known how sick Dad was, I would have been kinder to him.*

After Sunday lunch Dad asked Maisie to go for a walk. She hesitated. What on earth could they say to each other after their terrible conversation yesterday? But how could she refuse? She was so grateful that her father was alive that she would do anything he asked.

"Let's go somewhere we can talk," said Dad. He led her to the beach in front of the house. As she sat down on a log, Maisie braced herself. Was Dad going to scold her for what she had said?

"Maisie, I want to apologize. What you told me was perfectly right. I *haven't* been a good father. It was brave of you to say that."

She lifted her head. For the first time in months he looked directly at her. "It wasn't your fault," she muttered. "The war did it."

"Yes, it did. Something happened that I can never tell you, something that has changed me forever. But it's selfish to let that affect *you*. I'm sorry, Maisie. In the past six years I've neglected you shamefully, but I want to make that up to you. Shall we try again? You had something to say. I'm ready to listen—if you still want to tell me."

Why not? Maisie took a deep breath, then spilled it all out, pushing sand around with a stick as she spoke. Her tale seemed to go on forever.

"So now Una doesn't know that David is in love with her, and she's so miserable, and it's all my fault! I know I have to tell her, Dad . . ." Maisie was crying now. "But I just *can't*! What will she think of me, doing such a thing?"

Dad looked overwhelmed. Had she said too much? Could he cope with this in his still-fragile state? Worst of all, did he think his daughter was a terrible person?

He handed her his large handkerchief. "Oh, pickle, what a lot for you to bear! What you did was very wrong, of course, but you don't need me to tell you that. And of course you have to tell Una. I think she'll be angry at first, but then she'll forgive you. And maybe she and David will even end up together. That's a *happy* outcome, you know. Your granny has told me what a fine lad he is. You don't have to worry that you'll lose Una's friendship when she's with David. You two have always been so close— that's not going to end. And someday you, too, will meet a boy you love, and the four of you will be friends. I *hate* seeing you so unhappy. Tell Una right away, okay? Then you'll feel better."

He had his hand on her shoulder. His eyes looked tenderly into hers. He had called her "pickle." Was this really her distant dad?

"Okay," gulped Maisie. "I'll tell Una tonight. It'll be awful, but I'll do it!" Relief flooded through her, because she *knew* she would.

"That's my brave girl."

They sat in silence for a few minutes. Above them a raven chortled and croaked, as if it were encouraging Maisie to speak again.

"Dad?"

"Mmm?"

"What *did* happen to you during the war? What made you change so much?"

"I can't tell you, Maisie. You're too young to hear such things."

"I'm fourteen and a half! And I'd like to know, Dad . . . I really would."

"Well . . . I suppose I could tell you some of it."

Maisie listened intently.

"I was so impatient to get into the war," began Dad. "All my friends had gone over—Chester and fellows I knew from university. But they didn't take younger chaplains until after D-Day. Then I finally heard I would be sent to the Netherlands."

Maisie remembered Dad whooping when he'd received the letter. "But then you had to leave us!" she said.

"Yes, and of course I was sorry about that. But now I could do my bit, like everyone else. Pa was so proud of me. He gave me his travelling Communion kit, the one he had used when *he* was a chaplain, in the First World War."

"What does a chaplain *do*?"

"Well . . . many of the things I did at home. On Sundays I conducted services in a field or sometimes in a local church. I said prayers with wounded soldiers and last rites with dying ones. I buried many men, and I wrote letters to their families."

Maisie vaguely remembered Mum reading her this in Dad's early letters, but she hadn't paid much attention. The war had always been something that only the grown-ups worried about. It seemed more real now than it had then.

Dad had a faraway look. "I had to do much more than a rector's duties. I went along with the stretchers to bring back men and helped bind their wounds. Being on the battlefield was tricky with all the canals and dikes. Often I had to crawl on my hands and knees to reach a wounded soldier."

"That was *brave!*" said Maisie. "Grand says you must have seen some terrible things."

Her father grimaced. "Yes . . . much too terrible to ever tell you, as I've said. But sadly, I got used to them—most of us did. And I wasn't particularly brave, not nearly as brave as the men who were in actual combat. I just did my duty, but I think I was good at it, and the men seemed to like me. I tried to be a comfort, to jolly them along. They called me 'Chappie.' But then . . ." Dad's face filled with pain.

"You don't have to tell me," said Maisie quickly.

"Perhaps it would help me feel better if I did. Do you think you can handle it?"

She nodded, although she wondered if she could. Dad began talking again. Now his voice was strained.

"There was a young fellow named Johnny in the battalion, only eighteen or so. He'd been with them in Italy, where they'd seen some horrific fighting—some of the worst in the war. Johnny was a weedy chap, almost girlish. I don't know how he even got accepted as a soldier he had so little muscle on him. His most distinguishing feature was his big eyes—they were full of such misery. The other men avoided him."

"Why?"

"For—for reasons I can't tell you. Anyway, young Johnny came to me one day and asked to talk. Then I found out why he was in such despair."

Now Maisie didn't want to hear any more. But she had to keep listening, as her father's voice grew more and more anguished.

"He told me that his best friend had been killed in Ortona. Johnny had been very close to this fellow—in fact, he talked about him as if they had been brothers. He told me how hopeless he felt. He asked what the point of all this was. He broke down in tears he was so *desperate* for help and comfort and advice."

Dad's voice became bitter. "But I was no help at all. I just mouthed the usual clichés—that God was with him, that we all felt hopeless sometimes, that we were fighting to get rid of Hitler and just had to get on with it. I said a prayer with him and told him to carry on. I think—and this is the worst—I think I even despised him a little for his weakness of character."

Silence. Then, in wooden words, Dad continued. "The next day Johnny deliberately stood in the line of fire and was killed. Those of us who witnessed this hushed it up. I wrote to his parents and said he'd died valiantly, but he didn't—he took his own life. And it's all my fault! I should have seen how desperate he was. I could have had him sent away on leave because of battle fatigue. I *should* have. But I didn't."

"Oh, *Dad* . . ."

"So you see, Maisie, I was—I am—a complete failure as a rector. I thought I could carry on with that role when I returned, even though I was a fraud. For six years I crushed any thoughts about my role in Johnny's death. I thought I could force my guilt to disappear. But of course it didn't. It grew inside me like a festering wound until it had no choice but to burst. On Easter morning I couldn't play-act anymore. I lifted up the bread and wine, and all I could see was blood on my hands—Johnny's blood."

Dad began to sob. Huge, shaking, terrifying sobs, an ocean of tears. Maisie lifted one of his hands and held it tight, until the crying began to subside. She had never seen a man cry before . . . least of all her father.

"Oh, Dad—oh, my poor Dad . . ." she whispered. "Maybe it wasn't your fault. Maybe Johnny would have done it anyway, no matter what you said."

Her father looked up and grimaced. "I need that handkerchief back."

He mopped his wet face. "I don't think Johnny would have killed himself if I'd recommended that he go on leave. I'm not going to excuse myself—I was responsible for his death. And what I did—what I *didn't* do—means I can never go back to being a rector."

They sat in silence for a long time. Then Maisie had to ask a question.

"Dad?"

"Mmm?"

She took a deep breath. "Yesterday when you went for that long walk, were you—were you going to do what Johnny did? That's what they were all worried about."

"I won't lie to you, Maisie. After what you told me, I realized what a crummy father and husband I was. I felt utterly *useless*! I started walking, to where the road ends at Fowler Bay. I went down to the water, and for a moment or two I considered putting rocks in my pocket and walking into the sea and drowning— like that English writer did during the war. I thought I might end my life."

"But if you'd done that, it would have been all my fault!"

"Oh, pickle, is that what you've been thinking? It wouldn't have been at all your fault! Your words triggered my despair, but anything could have done that. There's something wrong with my mind right now, and that's nothing to do with you, Maisie. And I was only *considering* taking my life. I sometimes have, in these past dreary months. But then I remembered something."

"What?"

"I remembered that you needed me. That you asked me to help you and that perhaps I still could. It made such a difference. So you see, it wasn't your fault at all—it was just the reverse. By telling me the truth, you made me realize that I could try to be a real father."

Now it was Maisie's turn to cry. "You *are* . . . you're the same father you've always been!" she choked out.

"You know that's not true, pickle. Since I came back from the war, I've been a lousy father and a lousy husband. You and your mother expected me to be the same as before—but I had no energy left to feel anything."

He was looking away from her. Maisie longed to hug him, to comfort him and be comforted—but something in his rigid body told her he wasn't ready for that yet.

Then Maisie said slowly, "If it wasn't my fault that you thought of killing yourself . . . then it wasn't *your* fault that Johnny did! Don't you see? There must have been something wrong with his mind, too, something that the war did."

"It *was* my fault," said Dad again. "I didn't understand then that you *could* have something wrong with your mind—now I do. Now I understand Johnny's despair. But it's too late."

How bitter his voice was! He had retreated into his

darkness again, and Maisie couldn't think of any words to bring him back.

"Dad . . ." she finally ventured. "Couldn't you tell this to Grand? Maybe he could help you."

"No," said Dad firmly. "Pa keeps trying to have a talk with me, but I can't confess this to him. It would make him even more disappointed in me than he already is."

"But—"

Dad held up his hand. "We've discussed my troubles enough, pickle. I'm sorry I burdened you with them, but thank you for listening."

"Thank you for listening to *me*," whispered Maisie.

"You are welcome." He kissed her cheek. "Don't forget to tell Una. Now, let's go home to your mother."

CHAPTER FOURTEEN

Telling Una

After listening to Dad, Maisie didn't know if she had enough strength left to face Una. But she had to. She tried to believe Dad's words: that Una would eventually forgive her. But what if Una didn't?

"Let's go to the Hut," Maisie muttered after dinner.

They settled on the mattress, leaning against the wall. "Is anything the matter, George?" asked Una. "You look so strange!"

Maisie almost choked . . . how could she do this?

But she had to. "Una . . ." she whispered. "I've done something really wrong."

"What? Maisie, why do you look like that?"

Maisie had decided to start with the good part. She took a deep breath. "David *does* love you."

"David loves me?" Una cried. "How do you know?"

"I'll tell you. Will you just listen to it all before you say anything else?"

Una nodded, her face radiant. Maisie's heart lightened. No matter how much Una was going to hate her, at least Maisie had taken away her pain.

Maisie had rehearsed her confession so many times that her words came out like a swift volley of shots. "Before he left, David brought over a letter. He said not to give it to you until after he'd left. But I didn't—no, *please* don't say anything, Una! I read it, then I burned it in the stove. That's it—that's the terrible thing I did to you."

Una gasped. "You *burned* my *letter*?" She whirled to face Maisie. But why?" she croaked.

"I don't know. Something just came over me. I'm so, so sorry!"

Seldom had she seen Una look so fierce. She gripped Maisie's arm and ordered, "Tell me what he wrote. *Every word*."

Maisie took a paper out of her pocket. "I knew you'd ask me. I wrote down as much as I could remember."

Una snatched the paper and read it rapidly. "Oh, my David," she whispered. Then she looked up, and her rapture turned to anger.

"You hurt me, Maisie. You hurt me on purpose! I never want to speak to you again!"

"*Una . . .*"

But she had already fled.

⸎

Maisie was so empty of feeling she couldn't even cry. Dad had been wrong: Una would never forgive her.

She tried to console herself with the thought that Una now knew that David was in love with her. She would write to him immediately, of course, and tell him what Maisie had done. Then David would hate *her*, too. But at least David would know Una returned his affection. Perhaps one day they might end up together. Maisie hoped they would.

She really did! No longer did she want to keep Una from David. She loved her too much.

That's what puzzled her. That's what always had, especially this summer. *Why did she care for Una so much?*

She was Maisie's relative and her best friend, so of *course* she loved her! But Maisie knew in the deepest part of her that there was more to it than friendship. She felt . . . *romantic* about Una, the same way that Una felt about David.

But how could she feel this way about a *girl*? Anyway, what did it matter what Maisie felt about Una? Now she had lost her.

Maisie made herself return to the living room. Some of the family were sitting around the table, playing euchre.

Una, of course, wasn't there.

Dad was in a corner with the newspaper. He glanced up, and she went over to him.

"Did you tell her?" he whispered.

Maisie nodded. "She was furious. She said she never wanted to speak to me again!"

"Poor pickle. Don't worry, I'm sure she'll come round. Just give her time."

"Come and join us, chickie," called Granny.

Maisie hated euchre. She shook her head, said goodnight, and escaped to bed.

&

The next morning Maisie woke up to an unfamiliar sound: a steady, pounding noise like—

"Maisie, get up!" called Granny. "It's *raining*!"

Her voice was so urgent that Maisie dashed downstairs in her pyjamas. Granny took her hand and pulled her outside the kitchen door. They stood in the rain, their faces uplifted, and let the drops rinse them. The arbutus trunks gleamed with wetness, and the ground had turned to mud.

"Isn't it *marvellous*?" cried Granny. She stomped

in the puddles like a child. Then she grabbed Maisie's hands and danced her in a circle.

"Granny, I'm getting soaked!" complained Maisie. Her pyjamas were stuck to her like a clammy second skin.

"It's just the Lord's blessed water! But oh, all right, go inside and get dry. Wash your feet in the kitchen first."

Maisie did, then ran upstairs to change. She was glad it had finally rained, of course, but she felt the wetness far more than she felt Granny's joy.

At breakfast everyone was ecstatic. "It's the first time we've had a good soaking since May!" said Granny.

"It must have been the cloud seeding that did it," said Grand.

Even Dad seemed affected. He kept looking out the window and saying, "Your barrels will soon be full, Ma." The rest of the family smiled at him, rejoicing in his participation as much as in the rain.

All week Dad improved. He still spoke quietly and moved slowly, and he still spent much of his time sitting on the veranda. But he was coming back to them. He looked people in the eye, and he sometimes smiled.

Maisie was struggling to finish her bookcase. One afternoon Dad poked his head in and offered to help. His expert advice quickly solved all her problems with it; at last it was finished and ready to paint.

Dad even agreed to go fishing with Chester, and there was a gleam of pride in his eyes as he showed them the salmon he'd caught.

"It's a miracle!" Granny kept whispering.

"I think it's Maisie," said Mum. "It's all those walks you made him take, pickle. I couldn't persuade him to go outside at home, but you did! And something changed in him while he was alone."

"I just wish we knew what he's been in such a fash about. If only he would talk to Rand, but he still won't."

He's too ashamed, Maisie wanted to say, but of course she couldn't. Everything Dad had shared with her was a secret.

"He's agreed to talk to a psychiatrist, though," said Mum. "It's one Maud has found in Vancouver. We have an appointment for the middle of September."

"One of those head doctors?" Granny frowned. "Oh, I don't think Gregor needs *that.* He'll get well on his own. All he needs is good food and the love of his family, and he'll be fine."

"Gregor needs more help than *we* can offer him," said Mum gently.

Granny gave one of her disapproving sniffs, but she didn't say any more.

For the first time in her life Maisie looked forward
to leaving the island. She stuck close to her parents
and tried to act normal as they crammed the last treats
of the holidays into their final week. There were the
usual family picnics, plagued by wasps. There were
boat trips and hikes and meals. The heavy rain ended,
but the air was cool and the island fragrant with moist
earth, as if it were heaving a sigh of relief. The forest
trails were slippery with arbutus bark, and some of the
trees had started to change colour.

Una and Maud were present for all these occasions, of course. Sometimes Maisie tried to catch her
cousin's eye, but she looked away. Una carried *The
Day of the Locust*, one of the books David had recommended, everywhere she went. She seemed bot-
tled up with nervousness, always twitching her foot or
scratching the back of her neck—she must be waiting
for David's reply.

Ashdown Academy started later than Maisie's school,
so Una would still be on the island when David
wrote back. The next time Maisie saw her would be
at Christmas. Would she tell Maisie what David had
written? Or would she still not be speaking to her?

Maisie tried to care more about this, but she was
still numb. Maybe this was how Dad had felt these past
months: as wooden and lifeless as Clary's Pinocchio
doll. If so, he was even braver than when he'd crawled

through the battlefield to reach wounded soldiers. Now Maisie understood how hard he had found it even to get out of bed each morning.

No one noticed how detached and miserable she was, not even Mum or Granny. No one noticed that she and Una didn't communicate. There were too many people at every meal and on every excursion. Now Maisie really was an actor. She looked after Clary, and steered the gasboat, and helped Granny, and pretended that she was as carefree as the rest of the family.

Only Maud saw through her, giving Maisie odd looks from time to time.

Una must have told her, Maisie decided.

CHAPTER FIFTEEN

Another Secret

When Maud invited her to go to Walker Island for a picnic, Maisie knew she was in for a scolding. She didn't care: she *deserved* Maud's disapproval.

The current was strong, and Maud had to concentrate on steering the gasboat carefully across the pass. They tied the boat to the wharf, then walked a little ways to a grassy bluff. Once they had settled into a hollow in the warm rocks, Maud opened the picnic basket.

Maisie hadn't been here for years. How odd to see Kingfisher from another island! She gazed at the church and the rectory; she could even see Granny in the garden. It was as if she were observing her former happy life, one that seemed a very long time ago.

"Maisie . . ."

Maud's face was so serious that Maisie grabbed another sandwich.

"Mmm?"

"I'm sorry about what happened between you and Una."

"So she told you."

"She told me everything. All about David's kiss and him running away and about—well, about what you did."

A gush of hot tears melted Maisie's numbness. "Oh, Maud, I'm *so sorry*! I didn't mean to hurt Una so much!"

Maud hugged her. "Of course you didn't! It was very wrong of you, but you know that."

Maisie leaned against Maud's sturdy body and sobbed and sobbed. Finally she wiped her face with her napkin. "D-did Una hear from David?"

"I let her phone him. It's terribly expensive, of course, but I couldn't bear to see her in such suspense. They only talked briefly, but now she knows how David feels, and of course Una is totally besotted with him." Maud frowned. "I *totally* disapprove of this! Una is far too young to commit herself to anyone. I think David is latching on to her because he's so full of grief. I'd like to nip it in the bud right now, but they won't listen to me. So I've reiterated what David said. They are to stay apart until Una is eighteen, although they can write. Then they may see each other. I've tried to warn Una that they may not feel the same then. I told her that one or both of them may have met someone else. But of course she doesn't believe me." Maud sighed. "David is an awfully nice fellow, of course—if only Una wasn't so much younger. So much drama . . . how much easier it was when all of you were little!"

"Do you think Una will *ever* forgive me?" croaked Maisie.

"Of course she will! Just give her time. Next summer you'll be as good friends as ever."

Maisie's heart lightened. Maud was always right—surely she was about Una, as well.

Maybe now she could ask the question tormenting her. "Maud? Is there—is there something *wrong* with me?"

"What do you mean?"

"Well . . ." Maisie stared at the lively waves. "I don't know *why* I destroyed that letter! I don't know why I feel so strongly about Una. It's as if—as if I *love* her, the way she loves David! But that's not possible, of course."

Maud gave her a strange, careful look. "You and Una have *always* loved each other . . . ever since you were babies. You'd roll around on a blanket and poke each other and giggle. You're like sisters more than cousins."

"I don't think so. Una feels more than that to me. She feels like a—a *boyfriend*—except, she isn't a boy!" Maisie's cheeks burned. How could she utter such nonsense!

Maud was quiet for several long minutes. *She must really think I'm strange,* thought Maisie, trying not to cry again.

Then Maud sat up briskly. "Maisie, my love, there is *absolutely* nothing wrong with you, and in a moment I'll tell you why. But first I'm going to share a secret with you. No one else knows this—not even Una, although I'll tell her when she's older. But I think it's time for *you* to know. Do you swear never to share with anyone what I'm about to say?"

"Cross my heart and hope to die," said Maisie solemnly.

Maud laughed. "I once made Polly promise something by stabbing her finger and mine and then mingling our blood. I won't do that! Okay, here goes. What I'm going to say will shock you, but bear with me."

Maisie would never forget that conversation—the one that changed her life. As she listened, she crumbled dry grass in her hands. In the years to come, whenever she inhaled that sweet grassy fragrance it brought back Maud's words.

"Have you ever wondered why I don't have a man in my life?" Maud asked.

"Not really. I heard Granny say it's because you

were too hurt by . . ." She covered her mouth. *Oh, no!* Una had asked her not to tell!

"It's all right, Maisie. I know Una told you about Robert, and I don't mind. Aunt Jean thinks I'm not married because I was too hurt by him, right?"

"Yes."

"That's not why. I *do* have a relationship, but it's not with a man—it's with a woman."

"What do you mean?"

"I mean that sometimes women fall in love with other women—and men can be in love with other men—the way women and men love each other. Some people are what is called 'homosexual'—they are attracted to people who are the same sex they are."

Maisie's heart thudded. "But how *can* they be?"

"They just are. It's something you are born with, just as some people have red hair. But because that's not considered normal in our society, no one ever talks about it, so many people never realize that they're different. I *thought* I liked men—I was certainly attracted to Robert. But when I had sexual relations with a woman, I *knew* that my true desire was to be with one."

Maisie gaped. How could a woman have sex with a woman?

"Sorry, Maisie, that was a bit too much information for you. Don't think about the sex part. Most important is the love. Sylvia and I love each other. We want to be together always."

Sylvia! That was the friend Una had talked about, the one in Toronto who was once Maud and her mother's roommate.

Maud patted her arm. "All right so far? I know it's a lot to digest."

"I'm all right," said Maisie. "But I've never heard of this before!"

"That's because our society is so backward," said Maud bitterly. "Homosexuality is considered unnatural— in fact, for men, it's illegal! Sylvia and I have to keep our relationship a secret. If anyone knew, we'd be called 'deviants' or 'mentally diseased.' I would be disbarred from being a lawyer, and she would be fired from the university. I *hate* secrets—I always have. But this has to be one, just as I think Una has to keep it a secret at school that she's illegitimate. Maybe one day attitudes will change, but at the moment that's how things are."

They were silent for a few minutes while Maisie tried to take this in. Maud was in love with a woman! That meant . . .

Maud seemed to sense the revelation that was filling Maisie like warm, bubbly water. "Maisie, do you know why I decided to tell you this?" she asked gently.

"Maybe . . ." whispered Maisie. "Maybe you're telling me because . . . because I really *am* in love with Una. I kept the letter from Una because I wanted her for myself."

A kingfisher zoomed off the Walker Island wharf. "Oh, *Maud* . . ." It was as if all the pieces of one of Granny's puzzles were sliding into place at the same time. "It kind of . . . it kind of makes sense."

Maud smiled. "When Una told me what happened, it crossed my mind that you could be like me. In fact, I've wondered for several years if you are. But I wouldn't have told you if you hadn't brought it up yourself. You're still very young. You may love Una right now, but in a year or two you may love a boy. *It doesn't matter!* Someday you'll know for sure whether you prefer being with a woman, but it's far too early to decide that right now. Look how long it took me! I just don't want you to think that there's anything wrong with you. There isn't! It's perfectly *normal* for you to have feelings for my daughter. Can you believe that?"

Normal? She was *allowed* to love Una? Maisie felt rinsed, as when she had stood in the rain with Granny.

Then she remembered Una's angry words. "But she doesn't love me back."

"Oh, my poor Maisie! No, she doesn't love you in that way, although she certainly loves you dearly."

"She isn't even speaking to me!"

"She will. You shocked her by what you did, but just give her time."

Once again Maisie tried to cling to that hope. She gazed at a raven drumming its wings across the sky. It turned a complete somersault in the air before it soared away.

"Wow!" said Maud.

"I've never seen *that* before!" said Maisie.

Then Maud stood up. "We should get back before the tide turns. Are you all right?" she asked again. "This is so new for you. It's going to take a while for it to sink in."

Maisie's legs were quivering. But, for the first time all summer—perhaps for the first time in her whole life—she *was* all right.

"Remember this is *our* secret," said Maud as they got into the boat. Maisie grinned at her. It felt so important to have a secret that even Una didn't know.

CHAPTER SIXTEEN

The Kiss (2)

Maisie felt as raw as if she had shed a skin. Everything was in sharper focus—the dark firs against the sapphire sky, Grand's old hands like ripply mahogany, Clary's eyes as blue as her cornflower smock. It was as if Maisie's heart had turned a somersault like the raven.

Yet she still ached with the loss of Una. It was up to her cousin to make the first move, but she continued to avoid Maisie.

"Have you and Una had a tiff?" asked Granny. "She hasn't been over here lately."

"Of course we haven't," said Maisie carelessly. "She's just busy . . . practising. She's trying to learn a really hard piece before she goes back to school. And I've been busy painting your bookcase."

She lowered her face to hide her lie. At least in a few days Maisie would be gone—before the rest of the family noticed that she and Una weren't speaking.

On Labour Day Aunt Esther and Uncle Daniel had a lunch for Maisie and her parents. They were leaving on the afternoon steamer.

"How I hate it when you all start to go!" said Granny, as they walked to the hotel. "But at least I'll see your family at Thanksgiving, chickie. Maud and Una won't be here, though. Did you know they're going to Toronto?"

"Uh-huh."

What if Granny knew why? Had she and Grand ever heard of homosexuality? Probably not . . . they were much too old to know about such things.

"Are you looking forward to going back to school?" Grand asked.

Maisie shrugged. School seemed faraway and trivial. But at least it would be a rest from the intensity of the past few weeks. And she needed to be away from here, to have time to digest what Maud had told her, to take in the possibility Maud had revealed.

Maisie walked between her grandparents, swinging an arm of each. "I'll miss you so much!" she told them.

She noticed that Mum and Dad were also holding hands. Then Maisie *was* looking forward to going home. It would be different now, because Dad was so much better. He wasn't ready to search for another job, however.

"*I'll* get a job," Mum had announced yesterday. "Celia Partridge has been asking me for ages if I want to help in her craft store."

"That doesn't seem right," Dad had replied anxiously. "I should be supporting us."

Mum had smiled. "We can support each other. And I'm excited about having a real job—I never have! You two can take care of yourselves. After all, Maisie will be in high school, so she won't be coming home for lunch anymore."

High school . . . Maisie had almost forgotten that she'd be at a large new school next year. The same kids from junior high would attend, but there would be a whole new group from the surrounding countryside to meet, as well. That would be refreshing. And it would be easier to avoid Jim in a bigger school.

All through the farewell lunch she watched Una, storing up every detail until she saw her at Christmas. Una's long fingers automatically played tunes on the tablecloth. Her voice rang with joy as she joked with Polly.

That's because she was in love with David. What must it be like to have that security? To already know which person was the most important in the world to you?

Well, I know that, too! thought Maisie. But in her case, it wasn't reciprocated. Then she had to stop looking at Una, her heart hurt so much.

"Maisie?"

Una was speaking to her! Maisie was so shocked that she almost spit out her mouthful of cake.

"Do you—do you want to go for a walk? There's plenty of time before the steamer arrives."

"All right," muttered Maisie.

They thanked Aunt Esther and Uncle Daniel and went out into the sunshine. Una stumbled in her silly heels, until she took them off and left them on the side of the road to retrieve later.

"Are you still angry with me?" blurted out Maisie.

"I don't want to talk about it yet. Let's go to the beach."

Una led them down to the same cove—even the same log. *Not here!* thought Maisie, but she could never reveal that she had spied on them.

"I'm still a *little* angry, but not as much," said Una. She grinned. "It's hard to be mad when I'm so happy! And I need to talk to you. Oh, Maisie, I phoned David! He *does* love me! We have to wait three years before we see each other, but we can write. It's a kind of trial. I know we'll love each other even more when it's over. I bet we'll even get married one day! David didn't say anything about that, of course, because I'm so young—but I'm sure he feels the same."

Maisie wanted to remind her of Maud's doubts. But she couldn't spoil Una's utter belief in a fairy tale ending, not after what she'd already spoiled.

"Is *David* mad at me?" she asked.

"Well, not so much mad as surprised. He didn't understand why you did it, and I didn't know what to tell him." Una looked at her curiously. "Why *did* you burn the letter? Didn't you want me to be happy?"

What could she possibly answer? *Help me, God . . .*

"I—I just wanted you to myself, I guess," said Maisie. "We've always been such close friends, but if you were going to be with David that would change."

"But of course it won't! We'll *always* be friends! We're Nancy and George, right? Nothing has changed between us. And no matter what happens between David and me, nothing ever will!"

Everything had changed . . . but Maisie couldn't tell her that.

She gazed at Una's perfect face, at her smooth cheeks and rosy mouth. Now she understood exactly how David had felt, sitting on this same log—how he had found Una's beauty so irresistible that he couldn't help accepting her request for a kiss.

"Do you forgive me, then?" she whispered.

Una grinned. "Yes, I forgive you! You're my best friend!"

Maisie took a deep breath. She knew what she had to ask next.

"May I kiss you?"

"Of course!"

Maisie had kissed Una a thousand times before: hello kisses, goodbye kisses, goodnight kisses, all the ordinary kisses of family life . . .

This was different. She leaned over and pressed her lips firmly against Una's.

Una drew back in surprise. Then she giggled away whatever confusion she felt. "What a goose you are, George!" She went to the shore and began skipping stones.

"Someday you will know for sure," Maud had said. Maisie didn't have to wait for someday. She knew right now.

CHAPTER SEVENTEEN

A Year Later

Maisie stood on the deck of the steamer, waving good-bye. Mum and Dad had gone into the lounge to talk to a friend, but Maisie liked to linger as the island retreated behind her. She watched her family leave the wharf. Polly and Chester's new terrier was tugging Clary on its leash. Una's slim figure turned around and waved again. Maisie waved vigorously back.

The past two months had been calm and uneventful, even a bit boring at times: the kind of deliciously lazy summer when you sit on the veranda swing with a lemonade and a book and there's absolutely nothing you should be doing.

Maisie and Una's friendship was entirely restored. They never mentioned the burned letter. Una kept Maisie up to date on David, how he would be doing a fall internship at an observatory in California. To Maisie's relief, Una never told Maisie anything intimate from his letters. Every evening Una visited the log where she and David had kissed. She'd carved their initials in it.

In February the king had died, and Princess Elizabeth had become the new, young queen. Before that happened, Granny and Grand had actually met her! The dean of the cathedral had gotten them seats for the service the royal couple had attended last fall. After it there was a reception for a chosen few, including Maisie's grandparents.

Granny had curtsied (she'd practised for weeks), then shaken the royal hands. Princess Elizabeth and Prince Philip had each said "How do you do?" and moved on to the next person. That's all that had happened, but now Granny preserved in a special drawer the glove that royalty had touched. "When I met the queen" had become her constant phrase.

"You *didn't* meet the queen! She was only a princess then" was Mrs. Cunningham's retort.

But she couldn't deny that Granny had met the woman who was now the head of the Commonwealth. Nothing could top that. Until Mrs. Cunningham came up with something better, Granny was a queen in her own right—the queen of the island.

Even before Una turned sixteen, she asked Chester

to teach her how to drive. To Maisie's delight, she was included in the lessons. They borrowed Grand's ancient car and were allowed to drive it themselves— but only once a week because of the price of gas. Every Saturday morning they went on an excursion, taking turns at the wheel.

Maisie adored the feeling of control as she skil-fully shifted gears and steered the car along the bumpy roads. On the rare occasions another car or tractor or horse passed them Una would pull over in a panic, but if Maisie was at the wheel, she calmly drove on. She decided that if she ever earned enough money, the first thing she would purchase would be a car of her own.

In August Una had invited Hilda, from her class, to visit the island. Maisie asked her new friend Dien to stay, also. The four of them got on well. They spent the whole week building a tree fort for Clary. Maisie super-vised and was proud of how much she taught them.

Dien and her parents and brothers had moved to Canada from the Netherlands after the war. She and Maisie met in the first week of high school. Dien was strong and practical. Her family had a dairy farm outside of Duncan, and Maisie often spent the day there, helping to bring the cows back to the barn and milk them. Sometimes Dien told her what a terrible time her family had had in Holland before they left.

"We were so hungry we ate tulip bulbs!" she once said. Maisie listened in horror. What a safe war she'd experienced, in contrast to her friend!

Dien's parents had come for dinner and told Dad how grateful they were to the Canadians for liberating them. Dad had actually talked for a whole hour to them about the war.

Maisie was surprised at how much she enjoyed high school. There was much more variety in people and courses than there had been in junior high. At first she and Jim had avoided each other. Then Jim found a girlfriend, and he went back to his comfortable bantering with Maisie. He called her by her last name, as if she were one of the guys.

Maisie had talked the principal into letting her and Dien take shop, even though they were the only girls. She made a stool using a power saw. Mum was terrified that she'd slice off a finger, but Dad supported her. He gave Maisie free rein of his workshop, saying she now knew just as much as he did.

Once a month Dad travelled to Vancouver to meet with a psychiatrist. He gave Dad some pills that helped him stay calm. Maisie wondered if Dad had talked to him about Johnny. As far as she knew, he hadn't told Mum or Grand, and he didn't mention it to Maisie again.

After Christmas Dad began working part-time in the hardware store. Mum continued to work in the craft shop. They had moved from the rectory into a smaller house nearby. After rent there wasn't much money for extras, but Maisie didn't mind. She'd never cared about clothes, she could get books from the library, and they bought milk and butter from Dien's family at a lower price than at the store. Maisie had found an after-school job as a clerk in the grocery and was proud that she could contribute.

Maisie was relieved when her family began attending church again; it made their life more normal. The congregation was kind and accepting, and the new young rector started a youth group that Maisie attended. Maisie often brought up tricky questions about God. "You keep us on our toes!" the rector joked.

Maisie wore her secret like an invisible cloak in a fairy tale. It amazed her how differently she now looked at everything. When Betty or Lindy tried to get her to go with them to get their nails done, she just smiled and said she'd rather not. When her mother continued to despair at Maisie's refusal to wear dresses, Maisie didn't feel as guilty that she wasn't girlish enough. Perhaps one day she could tell Mum why.

Sometimes Maisie wondered if Dien was like her. She didn't seem at all interested in boys; all she cared about was her prize calf. She and Maisie were good pals, but Maisie was not drawn to her the way she was to Una.

Now whenever Una played "Be My Love," Maisie was just as moved by the lyrics as her friend was. *She loved Una.* At last Maisie accepted that. It didn't really help, though, because she would never receive any more from Una than friendship. Maisie kept reminding her longing heart that at least she had Una's companionship, that her cousin would always be in her life. She couldn't believe that she'd ever meet anyone else she loved as much.

When she told Maud that, she answered, "You will, Maisie. Just wait and see. People rarely stay with their first love."

"But look at Mum and Dad, and Polly and Chester!" *And Una and David,* she added to herself sadly. Una's utter conviction had convinced Maisie that she and David would end up together.

"You're right—but they're exceptions. I promise you that you'll meet someone else one day."

Maud was now as much of a rock to Maisie as she was to Una. This summer they'd had many illuminating conversations, in which Maud answered Maisie's shy questions. She said that she and Sylvia sometimes went to house parties in Toronto where they met women like them. "We were amazed to discover how many of us there are!" said Maud. "It's so confirming to know that we're not alone."

Whenever Maud assured Maisie that it was okay if she wasn't sure yet, Maisie just smiled quietly to herself. When she was an adult, Maud would fully accept her into this secret world.

Sometimes Maisie thought about how Johnny had loved his friend who had been killed. She wondered if he'd been like her and Maud. Maybe that was why the other men had spurned him.

The steamer rounded the corner, and Kingfisher Island was out of sight. The light had dimmed, and the air turned chilly, but Maisie stayed outside, gazing at the dark shapes of passing islands and the fiery-rimmed clouds.

Now she had only two more years of school! Mum and Dad were already talking about Maisie attending university in Vancouver. "You'll have to work hard and get a scholarship," Mum kept saying.

Maud had suggested that Maisie live with them while she and Una went to U.B.C. "It will save on expenses, and of course we'd both love to have you."

Una would probably be with David then. That would be too painful to observe every day. And besides, Maisie wouldn't be there. She hadn't yet gathered up the courage to tell the adults that she wasn't going to university at all—that she was going to be a carpenter! Her shop teacher, Mr. Dudik, knew a local woodworker who was willing to take on Maisie as an apprentice after she finished high school. This fall Mr. Dudik would introduce Maisie to him. She worried that she'd have to pay him. If so, how would her family come up with the money? Maybe she could carry on with her grocery job after she left school.

The years ahead were uncertain and scary. But Maisie always had the island. She still intended to live with Granny and Grand as soon as she could. The piney air and the sparkling sea and the love-filled refuge of the rectory were the foundation of her being.

Dad had announced at dinner last week that, in a year or two when he felt stronger, he wanted to take a course in something. War vets could go to college for free, so he could attend a trade school in Nanaimo.

"Maybe I'll become a butcher!" he joked.

Mum laughed. "Or a baker, or a candlestick maker!"

"Perhaps you'll even go back to the priesthood," said Grand quietly.

Dad smiled at his father. "Who knows? Anything could happen. I'm reinventing myself!"

So am I, thought Maisie.

ACKNOWLEDGEMENTS

Many thanks to my editor, Suzanne Sutherland, and my agent, Marie Campbell; to my former editors, Hadley Dyer and David Kilgour; to Ann Farris, Romilly Grauer, and the late Wendy Porteous, for their memories of the 1940s and 1950s; to Nancy Bond, Heather Maclean, Herbert O'Driscoll, and Susan Scott; and especially to Katherine Farris, my inspiration always.

Kingfisher Island, a fictional creation, is based on one of the Gulf Islands between Vancouver and Victoria.